BLOOD
MOON

BLOOD MOON

LUCY CUTHEW

WALKER
BOOKS

First published 2020 by Walker Books Ltd
87 Vauxhall Walk, London SE11 5HJ

2 4 6 8 10 9 7 5 3 1

This book has been typeset in Arial, DIN, Fairfield, Frutiger,
Futura, Helvetica Neue, Impact, Ubuntu, Verdana

Printed and bound by CPI Group (UK) Ltd, Croydon CR0 4YY

British Library Cataloguing in Publication Data:
a catalogue record for this book is
available from the British Library

ISBN 978-1-4063-9344-6

www.walker.co.uk

To Bronwen, Helen,
Kirsten and Rachel.

PART ONE

A SLICE OF NIGHT

I perch on the bench in
the planetarium staffroom
and take out my phone
with its smooth black and gold
star-spangled case and
read all the messages
from today while I wait
listening to the silent room,
checking it's empty
before I get changed.

There's a message from Dad
and a ton in the chat
with the girls called
BEANS ON TOAST
(the only thing
any of us can cook).

Dad
I will be the one in the
white ford behind the trees
at five past zero
hundred hours. D x

I think he's being *funny*,
but I don't get it.
He's on another planet.

At least he's agreed
to pick me and Harriet up
around the back,
and not *inside*
the ice rink,
like he wanted to.

I open BEANS ON TOAST.

Harriet
Just getting ready!!

Bethany
Remind me why we're going
to an *ICE RINK* birthday party.
Are we ten again?

Leylah
Apparently it's free cos
Jackson's on the ice hockey team,
but it's totally so he can show
off to everybody.

Harriet
He can show off to me.
Apparently he's amazing.

Bethany
I thought you fancied Lee?

Harriet
I can multitask.

Bethany

Lol.

I'm secretly quite up for it.

Marie

I'm openly up for it.

It'll be fun.

Harriet

What you all wearing?

Leylah

Shorts and a crop top...

And a massive hoody,

to get past the parent police.

Marie

Erm ... Ley, *ICE* skating...

I'm wearing two pairs of leggings

and a vest under my dress.

Leylah

Ugh. Changing now.

Warm clothes are so

unflattering on me.

At least I'll be allowed out.

Harriet

You always look lovely.

Has anyone heard

from Frankie today?

I finish typing,
then take off my uniform
and let my dress
slink down over my
not completely flat
(but also not yet
satisfactory) chest.

A dab of concealer,
a sweep of Benefit tint
on my cheeks
and I'm good to go.

Jackson Twigger's
Sweet Sixteenth
at the Ice Rink Disco.

(Although…
Jackson Twigger.
Sweet?
LOL.)

While I wait for the girls,
I scroll on my phone.
Harriet's posted a photo
of herself in our tree house.
#GettingReady #InstaMakeup
#Starlight #Stargazing #NightsOut

She looks really pretty,
her eyes all smoky,
but I know
the photo
is from
ages ago.

      It shouldn't annoy me,
      but we're *not* getting ready
      in our tree house tonight
      and I hate when
      she's being fake.

Under the photo
Jackson's replied,
ur hot.

Harriet's written
thanks babe and
done a winky face.

           (Does she actually like *him*
           or does she just like flirting?)

Harriet
We're here!
Bring it, biatch.

             I pull on my trainers,
             then open the door
             to the atrium

where Vidhi is
putting away a wooden box
of sparkling meteor rocks.

I wish I'd waited here
chatting to her
about astronomy
instead of looking
at what Harriet's posting.

"Have a good time,"
Vidhi says.
"You were great today.
You're clearly
really
into this."

"Thanks," I say,
her compliment
blazing inside me
incandescently.

"And send me
your application for the
summer programme.
Or you can
just bring it
next Saturday.
I'll make sure
Elaine gets it."

"Thanks," I say, again,
a flutter of nerves

at the thought of her
and the director
of this whole place
reading my essay.
"Thanks, Vidhi.
See you next Saturday."

"I'll be rooting for you!"
she says,
          which means
                    the World
                                        to me.

Vidhi did the exact same
summer programme when
she was sixteen,
and now she's got a
PhD in astronomy.
#LifeGoals

I push open
the double doors
and breathe in
the street-light night.
Over the buildings,
the crescent moon
is a sharp, bright slice
of other-worldly light.

I snap a quick picture.
The moon comes out tiny,
all of its majesty
lost by my phone's

complete inability
to take a picture of something
so far from me.

I know Harriet
will find it funny.

Me
Took this and thought of
you.
#ShitPicturesOfTheMoon

Harriet
LOL. Get your ass in here.
Skating's starting soon.

SWEET SIXTEEN

"Frankie!" Harriet screams,
waving at me,
bracelets jangling,
as I walk into the chilly
and unnecessarily
brightly lit room.

The music is loud,
and our crowd
spills out of a booth
near the rental boots.
I climb over the back
of the seats
and slide in between
Harriet and Marie.

Jackson is already strutting
in front of the group,
talking loudly
as though we're
his own personal audience.

There's Bethany,
      Leylah,
            Marie,
                  me,
            Harriet (laughing loudly),
      Dev,
Lee,
and Charlie.

Jackson is telling everyone
how last weekend
he got a new mountain bike
on his actual birthday.

He went out riding,
and met two girls
who were all over him
because
    chicks dig bikes.

Then he tells us how
he ended up
shagging
them both
as a birthday present.

                    (Yeah, right.)

He shows us all
a picture of him
straddling his bike,
with two girls kissing him,
one on each cheek.

                  "How long do we
          have to listen to this?"
              I mutter to Harriet,

but she doesn't
answer me,

and Jackson is still going,
gesticulating grotesquely
with his over-mobile groin.

Harriet grins at me
and fans her fanny
then rolls her eyes
like she's about to faint.

I whisper to Marie,
"Is it just me,
or is Jackson
disgusting?"

but Marie's not listening.

Then Jackson looks at me
scathingly.
Maybe he heard me.
I hope he did.

I don't care if he hates me.

Harriet's eyes stay
fixed on him.
Then she laughs
at something he says,
and throws back her head,
like a wolf howling at the moon.

As she does,
her tilted-back head
leaves a gap
under her chin and
I notice someone I hadn't
previously seen:
Benjamin Jones.

He's sitting between
Dev and Lee
in a leather jacket,
looking explosively cute.

He turns his eyes to me,
and right then
something physical
happens
down below.

He's so good-looking
I can feel the photons
bouncing off him
and colliding
with me.
#InstantCrush

NOTICING

The next time Harriet laughs,
mine and Benjamin's eyes meet
in the tiny bit of space–time
her thrown-back head creates.

I smile at him slightly.
He smiles back at me.

I don't know when
we last spoke
but recently I have noticed him
noticing me.

Only now it's not just
noticing each other,
or looking at each other.
We're really
seeing each other.

BLUSHING

"What are you
blushing about?"
Harriet's whisper
is like sandpaper
on my eardrum.

"I'm not!"
I squeak,
my voice high,
my larynx tight.

I thought she
was too busy
watching Jackson
to notice the colour
of my cheeks but

she's staring at me,
a single raised eyebrow
grilling me.

My cheeks grow redder
under the heat.

I could tell her
I'm giving Benjamin
the eye,

but I quite like
the privacy of

realizing
I fancy Benjamin
and not telling her.

I usually tell her
everything.

"Fine, ignore me,"
she says, clambering over me.
"I'm going to talk to Lee
while my hair still
looks amazing."

(Which one is it?
Jackson or Lee?)

Then she leans back in.
"By the way,
blushing fact:
apparently
it's not just your cheeks
the blood rushes to
when you're embarrassed.

It's your lady lips too."
She nods at my crotch
and grins

and I whack her.
"Harriet! Ugh.
You make everything
disgusting!"

"That's why you love me,"
she smirks
as she leaps off the bench,
sticks the landing,
and flicks her hair back
like she knows
she looks amazing.

Her skirt is hitched up,
stuck on her tights,

      and I try to tell her
     but the music is so loud.

       And anyway,
      right then I catch
     Benjamin's eye again
      and am presented,
        instantly,
     with confirmation
     of her blushing fact.

MILKSHAKE

Harriet squeezes on
to the end of the bench,
leaning in to whisper
something to Lee,
and pushing Benjamin
one person closer to me.
I listen to him
chatting to Dev,
wondering how
I might join in.

Then the waitress
brings our shakes.
No one can remember
who ordered which flavour
so she dumps them all
in the middle
and everyone *l e a n s*
across the table,
     milkshake spilling
     and finger licking.

I scrunch up my face
at the stickiness,
and pull my elbows away
from the mess.
Harriet catches me,
rolls her eyes at me.

Then slides the last shake
slowly towards her saying,
"Ooh, it's got a flake,
my absolute fave."

"Really," says Marie,
sarcastically.
"You never mention it."

Harriet nibbles
her chocolate gleefully
and finishes it
ridiculously quickly.

She licks her fingers
and shrugs as she says,
"I know what I like."

Jackson leans in and says,
   "Want some of mine?"
    and picks his flake
     off the top of his shake
     and leaving a trickle
      of strawberry syrup
       across the table
        offers it to Harriet
         to lick off the cream.

I turn to Marie,
so I don't have to see
Harriet's tongue
near Jackson's fingers.

(It's so unnecessary,
the
flirty,
touchy,
licky
publicness
of what they're doing.)

When I look back,
        Dev's getting up,

                    and

                        Benjamin

                                is
                                right next to me.

                        I sip my milkshake,
                            wondering how
                                to talk to him
                                without anyone
                                noticing.

                    And even though it's obscene,
                    I can't help wondering whether
                            he's watching as
                        I put my lips to my straw
                                and suck.

                        And there I go again.
                            I'm blushing,
                            but just then

Benjamin's arm
brushes my elbow

                                        and I'm about
                                        to speak when

the music gets louder
and Jackson shouts,
"Let's do this!"

Everyone stands up
to go and get hire skates
and our moment
is bro
        ken.

ON THE ICE

The girls and I
do swooping laps
under the disco ball,
which spins in circles,
shedding sparkles
in time with the beat.

We laugh at the boys,
who can't all skate,
and watch Jackson
zigzag backwards,
like the show-off he is,
pulling Harriet after him
holding her hands,
her hair flying behind her
and her laughter erupting
in flirty explosions
over the music.

And
        a l l   n i g h t
            I try to get
                near Benjamin.

                    Just
                    before midnight
                    the lights go low
                    and a slow

song comes on
and there he is,
in front of me.

"Hey," I say,
over the bass.
"How are you?"

"Good, thanks,"
he says,
sliding closer.
"You?"

"Good," I say.

Then he slips
and wobbles a bit
and his hands shoot out,
so I take his fingers
into my palm,
helping him
balance.

We're skin to skin.
His hands are warm.
And I'm worried
I'm going to say
something stupid,
or weird,

which is weird,
because *stupid*
is *so* not my thing,

so I say,
"Shall we skate?"

He nods and gives me
a sheepish grin.
"Sure thing."

And we drift apart a little bit
as we circle the rink,

and before I know it,
we're chatting,
and it's so easy.

"Do you normally come here
on a Saturday night?"

"No!" I say, laughing.
"I work at the planetarium,
then usually I go home
and Dad makes me
and Mum pizza
and we have a
movie night."

"Nice."

"What about you?
What do you
normally do?"

"Not this!" he admits,
slipping again

and tightening his grip
on my hand.
"I play rugby on
a Sunday morning
so I just get
an early night."

                    "Wild," I say, smiling
                    while trying to stop
                    picturing me and him
                    having a quiet night in.

"If I don't have rugby,
and I'm feeling really crazy,
I sometimes stay up
until, like, midnight,
watching science videos online."

                    "What kind of
                    stuff do you like?"

"Space stuff," he says.
"Mostly. Some of it
is so amazing."

                    I want to whisper
                    You're amazing,
                    but instead I say,
                    "Yeah, amazing."

DARK

**It's as
dark
as night
in here.**

And in the darkness,
no one can see
what you're doing,
or thinking.
And that
makes me
bold.

I slide along beside him,
our fingers touching,

         and just like that
         we're holding hands.

I glance around,
quickly checking
if anyone is watching,
but Harriet is with Jackson,
pushing Dev into Marie,
being so obvious it's cringey.
She doesn't see me.

The disco ball
rotates above us.
His face is speckled

with the silver flecks
of the turning light.

I want to say,
"I like your face,"
but instead I just blush
and breathe in

his leather jacket
and something sweet
like

"Cherry chapstick?"

"Huh?" he says.

"Are you wearing
lip balm?"

Benjamin chuckles,
and takes my arm
to draw me closer.
"Yes," he whispers.
"But don't tell anyone.
It's my sister's."

"Why are you
wearing it then?"
I tease.

"Because it's cold
and I've got chapped lips
and she left it
in my pocket."

"You share clothes with
your sister?"

He laughs. "We're close,"
he says and shrugs.
"And it's a great jacket."

                              "It is," I agree,
                              laughing as we
lap the rink,
        our arms going slack and taut
                    pulling one another closer and
                drifting away because of
                                    centrifugal force.

"Huh?" he shouts.
"What did you say?"

                              "Nothing."
                    I shake my head.
            My hair flies out behind me.
                    I feel like Beyoncé.

"You did!" he says,
 pulling me close again.
"You said *centrifugal*."

                              "Well, it is," I laugh,
                        although strictly speaking
                    centrifugal is a fictitious force,
                a mere explanation of a sensation.
                        But the music's too loud
                            to go into that now.

He laughs and suddenly
brakes with his skates,

swinging me around him,
demonstrating he
knows exactly
what I mean
by *centrifugal*.

                I take his other hand
                and twirl around him.

We stay like that
for what feels like
an eternity,
staring at each other,
until he pulls me in
           and—

                in my mind
                the word

       KISSING

          explodes like a supernova
            leaving a black hole,
            sucking everything in.

     Then suddenly
     the disco ball halts.
     The music stops.
     Our hands drop.

Midnight strikes.
The magic disperses.
And in the flight to escape
the bright electric light,
I lose Benjamin.

SMELLY FEET

We're just about to leave,
when Benjamin
comes up to me.

"Hey," he says.

> "Hey," I say, hoping the smell
> from my un-booted feet
> isn't wafting his way.
> (I've been at work all day.)

"I've got to go,
but it was fun
skating with you.
Thanks for helping me."

> I want to say something
> smart or witty,
> but I don't know *what*.
>
> "Yeah," I say, "it was, um…"

"Centrifugal?" he offers.

> I laugh, impressed,
> and a bit annoyed
> I didn't get there first.

"You're great on skates,
by the way,"
he adds, then grins
and walks away.

Leaving Harriet,
Marie, Bethany and Leylah
gawping at me.

BENJAMIN LIKES ME?

We say goodbye to the girls.
I walk out next to Harriet,
with smelly feet,
on cloud nine.

As we weave under
the acid-bright car park trees
to meet my dad,
Harriet goes on and on
about who likes who
and how Jackson
is so much nicer
when you talk to him
one on one.

Then she starts going on
about how Marie and Dev
would make a cute pair
if only they weren't both
so shy and how she's
going to try
to help Marie by getting
her to send Dev a
flirty selfie.

"Maybe I should do it for her?"

         "No," I say. "Don't.
            Just leave her."

"All right, all right," she says,

> while I'm thinking,
> *Don't ask about Benjamin.*

> I don't want her interfering.
> I want to keep it for me.

"So," she says.
"Benjamin Jones?
Would you?"

> "No," I reply quickly.

Harriet
wrinkles her nose and goes,
"Well, I reckon he's into *you.*
Do you want me to help you?"

> "No!"

"He's quite good-looking,
don't you think?"

> "Sure," I agree.
> #Understatement
> But I can't help
> smiling as I think
> about him.

Harriet gazes at me,
then pauses and
cocks her head.
"You look so pretty.
Smile like that again.
I'll take a picture of you."

> So I do.

GOSSIP

Dad picks Harriet and me up
around the back of the car wash
at five past twelve,
like he promised.

"Very cloak and dagger,"
he says, as I climb in the front.

Harriet tries to squeeze in the back,
but it's covered in Dad's biking crap.

"Sorry!" he says, reaching around
and shoving his stuff out of the way.
"I've been mountain biking today."

"Cool, where did you go?" Harriet asks,
like a massive suck-up,
giving Dad the cue to go into
way more detail than
anyone wanted him to.

"How was work?" Dad asks me.
"Did you talk about the form
for the summer placement?"

                                        "Mmm-hmm." I nod.

"What's that?" Harriet says.

"Oh, just that summer thing
at the planetarium.
It's kind of nerdy."

"Ooh, will you get one for me?
I've always thought
it sounded cool," she says,
more to Dad than me.

"You can just apply online," I say.
"I only picked a form up
because I was there today.
It's loads of work, you know?
You have to get a reference
from someone in astronomy.
And you need to be free
all summer."

"Imagine if we both got it!
It could be amazing.
You and me! Doing astronomy!"

"Yeah," I say, glancing
at Harriet in the back.
"That would be amazing."

"So, what about your night, girls?"
asks Dad. "Anyone *snog*?"

"Dad!" I groan.

"What?" he says. "I just want
a bit of gossip. Call it my fare.
Come on … who snogged who?"

"Ugh. No one calls it
snogging any more," I say.

"What do they call it?"

"*They* don't call it anything.
And *you* don't talk about it.
Don't even think about it.
We'd rather give you *money*
than gossip."

We're waiting
at a red light
when Harriet leans
into the middle,

and I glance at her face
glowing red
in the reflected light,

all confessional,
and she goes,
    "I didn't snog anyone,
    but Jackson did ask
    if he could message me."

"Gossip!" Dad squeals, clapping,
like he thinks he's one of us.
"You have always been
my favourite, Hairy."

"Traitor," I mutter.

Harriet ignores me.

THE TREE HOUSE

Mine and Harriet's telescope
lives in the tree house
between our gardens
where we used to

    have tea parties
        and make mud pies
            and rose perfume
            out of decomposing petals
            and mulchy leaves.

Now we stay up late, chatting
        and stargazing
            and taking photos of
             stars and
            planets and
        the moon.

Then we sneak to the baker's
to buy the first pastries,
before finally going
to sleep at dawn.

I'm knackered from
standing up talking all day
but Harriet wants
to go to the tree house,
and our parents say it's OK.

I move the telescope
to the waxing crescent moon:
a perfect sliver of possibility.

> "It's clear," I say to Harriet.
> "You should come and see."

But Harriet lies
on her back,
dangling her legs
over the edge,
making the canopy rustle
in the night breeze.

"I'm busy," she sighs,
her eyes on her phone

> missing the stars
> shining bright
> right above us.

TOP THREE

"Busy doing what?"

"Thinking about
Mr Number One,"
she says,
rolling onto her tummy
to face me.

Me and Harriet always
play Top Three.

The top three things we're
        thinking about,
        or worrying about,
        or obsessing about,

            on any given week
            or night
            or hour.

Harriet's top three recently?
Boys, boys, boys.

"Come on, then.
Who is he?"

"Actually,
there's a new entry…"
She sits up,

pulls her knees into her belly,
and performs a drum roll
on the floorboards
with her feet.
"At number one …
Professor Brian *Fox*."

"Ew!" I groan.
"Brian Cox is not a fox."

"Yes, he is. He is fit AF.
And he's clever.
I'm talking
major
  fanny
    flutters."

(Ugh.)

"I've been listening to
loads of his stuff recently."

"And me, for my application,"
I add, then immediately regret
mentioning it.

"Ooh! What do we have
to do for those again?"

"Write a long essay.
And get a glowing reference
from someone with evidence
of your passion for astronomy."
I know I'm making it sound hard.

"I was thinking of asking Mr B
to write one for me.
And to check my application."

"Oh, Mr B!
He's still top three."

"Please, Harry.
We've talked about this.
He's too old!
And he's a *teacher*."

"Oi! No judgement,
remember?"

"OK. Sorry.
Go on, then.
Let's have it.
Top three."

She puts down her phone
for a moment,
using her fingers
to check off her crushes.

"One, Prof Brian Fox.
Two, probably still Lee.
Three, Mr B …
   and his thighs."

Harriet lies back again,
picks up her phone,
and sighs.

"His *thighs*?" I cry.
"WTF?"

"Shh," she says, jabbing me.
"You're interrupting my fantasy.
He was taking PE on Friday.
Tiny shorts.

His thighs are
            unbelievably
                    meaty."

"MEATY?" I shout.
Then gag.
"Don't say *meaty*."

"Mmm," she sighs,
rubbing her thighs,
"meaty meaty *meaty*."

"What was he doing
taking PE?"

"I think he was subbing,"
she says to her phone.
"I'd sub for him any day."

"What does that even mean?"

"No idea,"
she says, giggling,
lifting her head up
and twisting to look at me.

"But he *is* dreamy."
She grins then
lies back again,

and I look down at her,
legs swinging
in the dark of the night,
stirring up the oily
scent of the tree.

"What about Jackson?"
I ask, to get away
from thinking about Mr B
in tiny shorts
and to stop her saying
the m-word again.
"Do you like him?"

"Kind of,"
she says, shrugging.
"We're messaging right now.
Shall I send him this?"
She turns her phone
to show me
a pouty,
booby
selfie.

"Oh my God!" I scream.
"You have no shame."

"Why should I?" she says.
"Come on, he's asking me
for a selfie."

"He'll show *everyone*.
Like he did with those girls."

"It's only a bit of bra.
You know, you can be
such a nun."

"Only compared to you," I snort.
"You've got the hots
for everyone."

"And you for no one."

I think about mentioning
Benjamin,
but she's still on about
her selfie, anyway.

"Maybe I won't send it.
It's not that flattering.
What do you really think?"

"Don't send it," I snap.
"Don't be so reckless."

"You're no fun any more!"
she grumbles,
and slaps her phone down
and flips over to look at me.

"What about you, O queen
of the parched vag?
What's your top three?"

Benjamin,
Benjamin,
Benjamin,
I think.

But I say,
"My essay,
my reference
and whether we'll get
that picture of
the blood moon
next week."

"Oh yeah, the blood moon!"
she cries, clapping her hands,
surprising me that she's
still excited about our
joint love of
astronomy
and photography.

I feel a bit bad that
I thought she wasn't
interested in anything
except boys.

"I've been researching
what we should do with
this blood moon.
I have loads of ideas
we can try."
She pulls out her phone
to show me.

"See this one," she says.
"Wouldn't the silhouette
of the tree look amazing?"

"Totally," I agree.
"I just hope
the sky is clear.
The forecast is really bad."

"Don't worry," she says.
"I just know it'll be
the perfect night."

I love how Harriet's
always so positive.
"I hope you're right."

"I'm *always* right."
She grins. "Now,
back to boys.
Tell me who you fancy.
Is it Benjamin?"

"No," I say,
a bit too quickly.

"Come on, I'm bored.
Give me something juicy."

"I have nothing juicy," I say.
"Although, maybe there's
something you can tell me…"

"Anything."

                              "OK ... so say I *did*
                                fancy somebody...
                                   Hypothetically.
                                 How would I know
                                      what to do,
                              you know, if I ended
                                    up *with* them,
                                      intimately?"

Harriet snorts. "Intimately,"
she says, doing a horribly
accurate impression of me.

Then she breathes out dreamily.
"Don't worry," she sighs.
"When you're with someone
you really like
you just k n o w what to do."

                                        "I believe
                                  that's true for you.
                       You're always so at ease talking
                              to somebody you fancy.
                            But you're so much more
                              confident than me."

"I'm not really," she says,
and for a moment she looks
kind of young.
Then she rolls back her shoulders
and pushes her chest out at me.

"I'm just faking it
until I start making it."
She pouts and waggles her
eyebrows at me.

"What does *that* even mean?"

"I don't know,"
she says, giggling,
then she gets up
and moves over
to the telescope.

"Right then, give us a look,"
she says, nudging me.
"And, Frankie,"
she adds, putting her face
to the eyepiece,
"if you do like someone,
just be yourself.
Yourself is lovely."

LITTLE LIES

On Sunday morning,
Harriet messages me
asking if she can use my printer,
under the pretence that mine is better
because you can print almost anything on it
including something
she says she needs for her French project,
but I know she wants to
          do homework
          together.

I'd rather do it
          on my own,
because lately,
Harriet is always
distracting me
or copying me,
or talking about
the latest person
she fancies.

I tell her she can use it later
because I'm going
to help Mum with work
at her lab,
and instead

I slip out of the house
and go down to the library
to work alone.

And while I work
I think about the possibility
of Benjamin
popping in to get something
and coming over to talk to me.
Or sitting opposite me,
and us doing our
homework together
and talking
passionately
about physics and stuff
because Benjamin
is sciency like me
and maybe us
ending up
in between two quiet shelves
kissing or something.
#Hypocrisy

NON-SCHOOL-UNIFORM DAY

Harriet opens her front door
wearing a low-cut T-shirt,
reeking of perfume,
and with so much makeup on
I wonder for a second
if it's Saturday,
not Monday.

"You're not going to school
like that, are you?" I ask,
before I can stop myself.
"We're not allowed makeup."

"Good morning to you too,"
she says, rolling her eyes.
"We're not in uniform.
I can wear what I like.
Anyway, it's the *natural look*."

"RuPaul style."

"Frankie,
in case you've forgotten,
we're allowed to dress
however we want today."

"I don't think that"
– I point at her outfit –

"is what they meant.
You're going to
get into trouble."
Why does she have to
be so reckless?

I wonder whether she's
dressed like this for Mr B.
I still can't believe
she fancies him.

"For what?
Wearing a T-shirt?
Come off it.
Still rocking the nun vibe,
I see," she says, taking in
my skinny jeans
and retro NASA hoody,

which I was hoping
made me look clever
rather than nunny.

"If nuns can be astronomers,
then sure," I say, laughing it off,
but wishing I'd worn
just a bit of makeup
for non-school-uniform day.
I wonder if I'll see
Benjamin today.

Just then, Harriet's mum
comes out of their kitchen,
drinking a green smoothie,

her slinky dressing gown
sliding over
her bare legs.

"Bye, girls," she calls
as she heads upstairs.
"Give 'em hell."

DISTRACTIONS

Our year is gathered
for assembly
in the auditorium
with the head.

The audience lights are
on and Mr Adamson
is going on
and on
about (the girls')
school uniform.
#We'veHeardThisOneBefore

"We must eliminate distractions
to your education.
Exams are soon.
I don't want anyone failing.
  I don't want to see
    short skirts …"

                                        (he says this to
                                            three girls
                                        in the front row)

          "hair dye …"

                                        (to Bethany,
                                    who has dyed hers
                                        bright blue)
          "or inappropriate makeup."

                                        (to Harriet).
"They are all distracting."

"For who?" Harriet hisses in my ear.
"Him? The crusty old perv."

I wish she'd stop
drawing attention
to herself,
but she does have a point.
I'm not sure who
is going to find it hard
to concentrate in class
because of Bethany's
cobalt-blue bob.

And if anyone does,
I can't help thinking
that's their problem.

I glance around the room,
wondering where Benjamin
normally sits in assembly.

Right at the end,
I spot him,
a few rows
in front.

He doesn't see me.

SHAMELESS

Mr Adamson pushes past us
as we leave assembly.
"Excuse me, ladies."

                              "Sorry, sir," I say,
                      moving out of his way.

Harriet flutters her lashes
at his back and says,
"I hope I don't make anyone
think about anything
uneducational today."

                              "Harriet!" I hiss.
                      She's so reckless.

"What?" she says.
"That git has the nerve
to suggest that my makeup
might make someone fail
their exams.
I'm not having it."

                              "You are shameless."

"And you're a coward.
You hate him
as much as I do.
Don't pretend

you respect him.
'Sorry, sir!'" she says,
doing a mean impression of me.

Then she trots off
to catch up with Leylah
and Bethany, saying,
"Did your dad go mad
about your hair?"

But before they're too far away,
she turns around, hands in prayer,
and says, "See you in physics,
Sister Frankie."

CHANGES

Me and Harriet
have been besties
since I can remember.

When
we were in year two,
in Mr Parlow's class,
literally *everything*
was a laugh.

I wish we could go back
to being silly all the time,
but the feeling of it,
the freeness of it,
has gone.

I wish Harriet would stop
reminding me
I'm not as fun as I
used to be.

Although now I wonder
if I was ever as free
as she seems to be.

CHANCES

Harriet wants to sit at the front
of the physics lab,
probably so that Mr B
can see her smoky eyes,

but it suits me
because I want to know
if he got my email asking him
to write a reference for me.

"Today, we're looking at
weight and mass," he says.
"Settle down now,
let gravity guide you
to your seats, ha ha."

Harriet laughs really loudly.

All through class
I scribble madly,
taking in every word
he says

while Harriet drops her pen
every five minutes
and struts to get it,
bending over
  o u t r a g e o u s l y   s l o w l y
right in front of Mr B.

Before we leave,
he intercepts me at the door.

"I'll write your reference
and give it to you Friday.
Do you want me to
read your application too?"

                              "Yes, please," I say.

"I think you have
a really good chance,"
he adds.

                         I feel my face flush
                 with pride that he has recognized
                       this is *my* special thing.

                              "I'll email it later.
                                 Is that OK?"

"Absolutely," Mr B says.
"Nice hoody, by the way."

Behind me I hear Harriet say,
"Can you read mine too, sir?"

"Of course."
But then he says,
"You have it now?
OK, stay behind.
I'll take a look at it
right away."

I hear her say,
"I just love the stars…"
but I have to move to let
the rest of the class
file out.

So it's from outside
that I watch her
lean over his desk

                              (so inappropriately)

while he reads
her application

                              before mine.

WE'D BE ALL RIGHT

No chance of stars,
it's raining,
but even so
Harriet and I
go up to
the tree house
after dark.

"So did Mr B
like your application?" I ask,
while she gets her laptop
out of her bag.

"Yeah," she answers, vaguely.

"What did he say?" I ask,
wondering if
he thinks she's got a
really good chance.

"Oh, you know."

"No," I say. "What?
Did he read your essay?
Did he suggest any changes?
Did he think it was a good topic?"

"Frankie, can we
just leave it?"

69

"Sorry," I say.
If it were me
I'd want to talk about
it all evening.
"I was just asking."

Harriet scowls at me.
"Look, we're not all
Mr B's favourite,
you massive physics nerd,
so it wasn't exactly a shower
of glory. And I don't feel
like talking about it.
Least of all to you."

"I'm sure yours is brilliant,"
I say, trying to sound
encouraging
but realizing I probably sound
patronizing.

She's on her phone
so I set up the laptop
and wait for her

as she laughs
then sighs about something.

"What's up?" I ask lightly,
hoping we can
change the tone.

"It's Jackson," she says.
"He won't stop messaging."

"I thought you liked him?"

"I did," she says. "But now
it's getting kind of boring."

"I told you not
to get involved."

"No, you didn't.
And now he's obsessed.
And you know
he told us he got with
those two girls that night?
They're his cousins!"

I burst out laughing.
"That's incest."

Harriet whacks me.
"Obviously nothing happened.
He lied to brag.
I'm not into that,
know what I mean?"

"Totally," I say.
But I want to stop talking
about Jackson and get on
with our evening.

"How do I get rid of him?"

"Tell him you don't like him?"

"Ooh," she says, typing,
"I'll tell him I'm busy
and I'm going out with you."

               "Harry," I say. "That's lying!
                     Just tell the truth.
                And then can we please
            watch *The Walking Dead*?"

"Absolutely," she says,
hitting *send*
and then turning her screen
to show me.

She has actually written
that she's *with me* with me
and not to contact her again
because of my jealousy.

                    "Harry!" I gasp.
                 "You're such a liar."

"It's fine," she says.
"Everyone lies a bit.
He'll know what it means.
I'm saving him face."

                    I'm just glad
              she's not taking things
            any further with him.

She tucks her phone away
and pulls the snacks out

of her backpack
then opens her laptop
and presses *play*.

We nestle into the pile of pillows
and with the fairy lights twinkling,
and us alternating eating
tortilla chips and tangerines,
we spend the evening
scream-laughing at the
incompetence of everyone
   except Rick Grimes.

                     (Actual fanny flutters.)

"You're drooling!"

                            "Am not."

"You can't have the hots
for Rick, and tell me
Mr B is old."

                      "Different rules
                  for the apocalypse."

"Stab it!"
Harriet says.
"You idiot."

                  "Shut the door!" I yell.

"Use the machete!"
Harriet shouts.

                                        "Run away!" I scream.

"Use the machine guns!"
Harriet says.

                              "Lock the doors and hide!"
                                        I say, feeling safe

                    up here, in our tree house,
                    where no one can get us,

                    watching other people
                          being useless,
                    and knowing, if it was us,

                          we'd be all right.

                                        Well, honestly,
                                        I'd be scared shitless.

But Harriet
is actually pretty brave.

LUNCHTIME

In the lunch hall
I subtly scan the room
for Benjamin,
before I pick a table
and start to eat
my saucy spaghetti
(carefully,
in case Benjamin's watching me).

Harriet sits down heavily
and sips her large
black coffee.
"Ugh." She shudders,
swallowing and grimacing.
"This is so bitter.
It's disgusting."

"Why're you drinking it then?"
laughs Leylah,
opening a can
of lemonade.

"Because I'm dying," Harriet says.
"I didn't go to sleep until 4 a.m."

"Sexting Jackson?"
Bethany smirks, nudging Harriet.

"I told you," she says,
   leaning away from Bethany,
"I ended it with him.
And your lunch
   absolutely stinks."

"All right," grumbles Bethany.
"Don't have a go at me."

"I'm sorry," says Harriet,
   rubbing her hands over her face
   and groaning. "I'm just so tired."

                    "What were you even doing?"
                       I ask. "I was with you
                          until about ten."

"I was rewriting
   my application to
   send to Mr B."

                          "Oh," I say.
                 I feel a pang of jealousy.
                    What if she worked
             on hers harder than I did?
                    "Did you manage it?"

"Just," she says. "I sent it
   this morning then had
   about two hours' sleep.
   But I think I made
   a horrible mistake."

"What?" I ask.

"No," says Harriet. "I'm not telling you.
It's too embarrassing."
She groans
and folds her body forward,
resting her forehead
on the table.

Marie says,
"Nothing good gets done
after 10 p.m., if you ask me."

"Well, I didn't," Harriet retorts
from under her hair.

"I'm sure it's not as bad
as you're imagining,"
says Leylah.

"What if it's worse?"
Harriet mumbles.

I try to think of
something reassuring
to say but just then

I see Benjamin
walking towards me
and I'm briefly distracted,
wiping my face
and smiling at him.

                                        He grins at me
                                        as he walks past.
                                        God, he's dreamy.

When I look back,
Bethany is patting Harriet's head.
"I'm sure it's great."

"You'll feel better
 after a good night's rest,"
 says Marie.

"Enough with the sleep, Marie,"
 Harriet moans.
"And, Beth," she adds,
"you had better
 not be getting
 tuna in my hair.
 It took me an hour
 this morning."

And we all giggle
as Bethany licks
her fingers
quickly
before resuming her patting.

EXTRACTION

That afternoon, in history,
a year seven
knocks on the open door,
a piece of paper
trembling in her hand.
"I have a message
from Mr Adamson."

Ms Wyse
beckons the girl,
lowers her glasses,
reads the note,
and sighs.
"Harriet Prosser,
you're to go."

Harriet glances at me.
She looks worried.
Then she gets up
and slopes off
out of the door
and as I hear her footsteps
fade down the hall
my stomach knots.

What's she done?

DISTRACTIONS

Mr Adamson banged on about distractions
for about an hour just
yesterday.

I can't think of many things more distracting
than extracting someone in the middle of class
with no explanation.

Apparently Mr Adamson's
second lesson of the week is
irony.

SPECULATION

After Harriet goes
we're meant to be reading in silence
but everyone is whispering
and the boys are all giggling.
I can tell
that something
is going around.

I remember once,
when Mohammed's mum had a baby,
he got to leave early.

Another time, Caylee's grandmother
was in hospital dying,
and she was called out of class.
Apparently she only just made it
in time to say goodbye.

Births and deaths.
What could be dramatic enough
to warrant Harriet's extraction?

Everyone has a theory,
but I know it's about
what she mentioned at lunch.
The thing she wouldn't tell me.

I put her bag in her locker
when we leave the lesson

but then in the corridor
between classes
I hear Harriet's
name behind me
and turn to see
Jackson, Dev and Charlie
laughing and whooping,
their necks craning
around Harriet's phone,
taking pictures
with their phones
of her screen.

I push myself
in to see an email
Harriet has sent.

To Mr B.

                                "How did you get that?"
                                        I snap,
                snatching her phone
                                off the boys
                        and tucking it in my pocket.
                                "You can't just take
                        things out of people's bags!"

"It fell out of her bag in class," says Jackson,
 holding his hands up.
"I was just looking after it,
 as *you* didn't notice."

                                "Bullshit," I snarl.
                                "How did you open it?"

"Nine nine nine nine
is pretty easy to see
when you sit behind
somebody."
He snorts, looking between
Dev and Charlie, adding,
"Easy. Lol. Just like her."

God, he's disgusting.
"You'd better not have
done anything,"
I say, turning away

and leaving them
whooping and
calling after me
to lighten up.
Down the corridor,
I look at her screen
and read

the email.

She's sent him her
application again,
and she's attached a selfie.

She's in bed wearing
a low-cut pyjama top
and she's leaning in,
her boobs squeezed.
She's written:
Hopefully you'll agree
I've worked really hard on this.
Can you check it over again?

Ugh, Harriet.
I cannot believe her.
Doesn't she ever think
about the consequences
before doing something?

TROUBLE

I sit in geography,
worrying.
Harriet's going to be
in so much trouble.
You can't send a picture
like that to a teacher
and get away with it.
What was she thinking?

                    I check my phone
                    under the table,
              unable to concentrate
                    and wondering
                    what's happening
                    to her now.

Mr B must have told the head.
They might suspend her.
What if they expel her?

                    I don't know whether to cry
                    or scream.

Then
an unknown number
messages me.

In iso. Meet me
in the toilet in ten.
H

I wait in geography
for nine minutes,
feeling sick, finding it
impossible to concentrate
on anything Miss Allison says,
which is annoying because
she's already told us
tectonic activity
will be in
our mock exam.

Finally, it's time.
I slip Harriet's phone
out of my bag
and into my pocket
next to mine.
I walk to the front
and ask for a pass
to go to the loo.

Miss Allison
looks at me
suspiciously.
"Quickly then,"
she says, like she knows
I'm up to something.
"Five minutes,
or I'll come check on you."

FIGHT

I hurry down
the silent corridor,
Miss Allison's threat
following me.
Five minutes.
If she checks up on me
they'll find Harry too.
(Meeting someone
while skipping isolation
got Joseph Carlton
a month-long exclusion.)

The toilet door
bangs shut behind me
making me jump.
I'm so worried
I'm already sweating.

"Harriet?" I whisper,
peering around
cubicle doors.

A hollow sniff echoes
from the last stall.

Harriet's perched on
the toilet seat.
Black mascara streaks
her cheeks.

Once in primary school
Harriet hid in the toilets
because Lena Kowalski
said her head was too small
and we ended up laughing
about it.

I don't think laughter
can help us now.

I crouch down next to her,
hug her,
squeeze her
trembling body.
"Oh, Harry," I sigh.

What else can I say?

"Frankie," she sobs,
practically hyperventilating.
"I'm in so much trouble."

"Why are you out of iso,
and whose phone did you
text me from?" I ask her,
checking over my shoulder,
hoping nobody else comes in.

But she's crying so much,
I can't understand
what she's saying,
and her sobs are echoing
all around the toilets.

"Shh," I hiss, ripping off some toilet roll,
checking the time as I wind
the paper around my hand.
I've already been gone
two minutes.

"Just breathe," I tell her.

Harriet sits up and
blows her nose,
then turns around
and lifts the lid
of the sanitary bin
and quickly throws
the soggy clod in.

I sweep my thumbs
under her eyes
to dry her tears
and clean her face.

"Don't judge me,
Frankie," she says.
"But I sent something
I shouldn't have."

"I know," I say. "I've already seen."
I take her phone from my pocket
and put it on her knee.
"Jackson had it.
He saw your passcode
over your shoulder.

They took a copy.
I'm really sorry."

"Ugh," she moans.
"So embarrassing.
And Mr Adamson had
such a go at me.
He says I'm getting
detention all week."

"Well, that's not surprising."

Harriet looks up and
narrows her eyes at me.

"Sorry," I say.
"What are you going to do?"

"I was thinking … maybe
I can say I didn't send it?"

"Or you could take some
responsibility?"
It comes out
before I can stop myself.

"Thanks, Frankie," she says.

"All right," I say,
holding my hands up.
"I just don't think
you should start lying."

"I can't believe Mr B told on me!
Mr Adamson said
the photo might be classed
as *child pornography*."

"Oh my God! Harry!
Do you not think
that's *why* he told on you?"

"Calm down, Frankie,"
Harriet says, flippantly.
"It's just a tiny bit of tit.
There's no way Mr Adamson
will call the police.
He's exaggerating
to scare me."

I check the time.
I've been gone four
minutes.
#ShitShitShit
"It's not *just tit*.
Don't you get it?
This is serious.
What is Mr B going to
think of me?"

"What's it got
to do with you?"

"Everything!" I spit,
forgetting to whisper.
"I'm your best friend.

He knows we're
always together.
He's going to think
I endorsed it!"

"Oh my God," she says.
"*Endorsed it…*
Get over yourself!"

"Me? What's got into
you lately?
You need to
take this seriously!"

Harriet's tears have stopped.
She stares at me coldly.
Her mascara is gone,
her foundation too.
Her freckles are showing
like they always used to
when we were little
before she wore makeup

only I don't recognize
who she is any more.

"I *am* taking it seriously,"
she protests.
"Why do you think
I was so depressed at lunch?
I know it was stupid."

"You're not taking
anything seriously.

92

You're all over the place
chasing Lee,
texting Jackson,
dumping Jackson."

I have less than one
minute to get back to class
before Miss Allison comes.

"And now sending Mr B
that slutty selfie!"

"Slutty?" she screams.
"Fucking hell, Frankie!
You think you're
SOOOO
PERFECT!"

"Harriet!" I snap. "Shut up!
Or we'll both get busted."

"Oh, and if *Saint Frankie* got
into trouble, *that* would be
the end of the world."

"Hey," I say. "That is *not fair.*
I don't want to be here."

"Then don't be," she shouts,
shoving past me.
"You're not helping me;
you're just judging me!"

I reach out to stop her,
but she flings me
off her

so violently
I slip on the tiles
and fall to the floor.

I stare at her,
pain exploding
in my hip where I landed,
and in that moment
I hate every bone
in her body.

She spins around
and looks at me
and I see in her eyes
that she hates me too.

She moves and I think
she's going to hit me.
"I am
done with you,"
she spits.

"You're NOTHING TO ME!"

"Good!" I shout.
"I don't want to be
friends with
a slut anyway!"

She storms to the door,
opens it and shouts
into the corridor,
"FRANKIE YOUNG IS
SKIVING IN THE TOILETS,
BUT I MADE HER DO IT."

She looks down
at me on the floor,
and whispers,
"Happy now?"
then whips her hair
over her shoulder
and struts out.

HAPPY?

I'm terrified
a teacher
heard and I might
get detention,
or worse.

I'm furious
she deliberately
tried to get me
into trouble.

I'm hurting
where I fell
when she
pushed me.

I'm worried
she might
get into trouble
with the police
or Mr B might
lose his job.

I'm frustrated
with her
for not taking
anything seriously.

And I'm aching
inside more
than I could
ever have imagined
at hearing her say,
"You're nothing to me."

Those words
echo inside me
making me feel empty.

Nothing to me.
        Nothing to me.
                Nothing to me.

                        No. I'm not happy.

LATER

Harriet isn't
at the gate
after school.

I walk home
alone,
seething,

and even though
she shouted at me
that I'm nothing to her

I'm still not quite
angry enough
not to miss her,
just slightly.

TALKING

That evening,
I try not to look at my phone.
Harriet can deal with
this on her own.

She doesn't want me.
She said I'm nothing
to her.

I go to the living room
with a heavy feeling
and a tummy ache
to half watch *Bake Off*
with Mum and Dad,
a physics textbook
open on my lap.

"Are you OK?" asks Mum,
looking up from
a pile of marking.

"No," I say.
"I hate everyone
and everything."

"PMT?" says Mum.

"Maybe," I reply
gloomily.

"Cuddle?" offers Dad.
"You're not doing homework.
You haven't turned the page
for about three cakes."

              "No, thanks," I say,
          ignoring Dad's hurt face.
          "Me and Harriet had a fight."

"Have you tried talking about it?"
Mum asks, taking off her glasses.

                    "Ugh," I say.
                    "We're way
                    past talking."

"You said that last time."
Dad mutes the telly, and crosses
his legs to face me.
"Come on, talk to *us*."

                    "No," I say.
                "I don't want you
              to be all reasonable
              and understanding.
                  She's a bitch."

"Language," tuts Mum,
putting her marking aside.

But Dad pouts sassily,
then flicks his non-existent
hair over his shoulder

and squeals,
"Tell me she did not snog
that boy I fancy?
I'll *kill* her if she even
looks at him
one
more
time!"

                              "Ergh, Dad! Stop it.
                                  And I told you,
                                     no one says
                                 snog any more."

"Pash?" he tries.
"Smooch?
French ki—"

                                          "Dad!"

"Come on, Frankie,"
says Mum, tucking her
hair behind her ears.
"What did Harry do?"

                               I shake my head.
                                I can't tell them.

                             It's too embarrassing.
                              What if they think
                            that's the kind of thing
                                we're all doing?

"Well, we're always here
  if you want to talk," says Mum,
  putting her glasses back on.

*"You just call
    out my name…"*
Dad starts to sing.

                                        "DAD!" I start,

but Mum gives him a
serious look over the top
of her glasses and he stops,
acting out zipping his lips.

                        "Thank you," I say to her.

"At your service," replies Mum,
  going back to her marking.
"But you should talk about it,"
  she adds, without looking up.
"Talking always makes it better.
  Sometimes worse first.
  But always better in the end."

                        "Yeah, yeah," I say.
                        I've heard it before.

"Listen to your mother,"
  Dad mumbles
  out of the side
  of his mouth.
"She is very wise."
Then he unmutes the telly.

EXPLOSION

When I go up to bed
and I'm finally alone
I can't help check my phone.
BEANS ON TOAST
has exploded:
a hundred and
fifty-eight messages.

Harriet's flapping
because the whole
school knows she
basically sexted Mr B.

I only skim read.

The girls all share screenshots
of what everyone's saying
in other groups
so that Harriet can see
and they can help
her be outraged
about Mr B telling on her.

(Instead of addressing
the real problem,
which is Harriet
not taking responsibility
for her own stupidity.)

And then I see
they're all saying
they've seen the picture
and they don't think

she's a *slut*.

My stomach sinks.
My insides shrink.

She's turned
them against me.
She's told them
about our fight
and what I said
and they've decided
Harriet's right.
#TakingSides

I go to the bathroom
to brush my teeth
and through a crack
in the open sash window
I can hear Harriet crying.

When we were little
we used to do bird calls
through these exact windows
late at night
if we wanted to speak.

We'd sit on the sills
and chat until
one of our parents

caught us and told us
it was time to go to sleep.

I listen to Harriet weep.
I'm so
angry with her
for shouting at me
pushing me
for trying to get me
into trouble today
for saying
"You're nothing to me"
that
I cannot say
~~that I care about her~~
~~that I don't want her to be hurt~~
~~that she's **everything** to me~~
~~how she's my best friend~~
~~and I love her~~
anything.

I close the bathroom
door behind me
and get into bed,
pulling the covers
up around me,
salty anger spilling
onto my sheets.

It takes me
ages
to fall asleep.

THIGHS

I can't remember when
I last walked to school
without Harriet.
We've walked together
since we were ten
and before that
literally every day
with my dad on his way
to work at the bike shop.

Sometimes he used to
let us take it in turns to
sit on his saddle and
he'd wheel us along,
deliberately wobbling
with us giggling.

I slip out quickly,
avoiding Mum, and I
go the long way so I don't
have to pass Harriet's house.
There's no way
we're walking together today.
I don't even want to see her.

The streets are slow
without any gossip.

I've only walked down
three and already it feels
like it's taking an eternity.

But as I turn down
the next street,
I see Benjamin
closing his front gate.

Perhaps he's been
walking this way
since we were in
primary school,
and I never knew.

He's so hot.
(And so cool.)

I push thoughts of
Harriet aside, and
pull myself up tall,
set my eyes
to the parting clouds
like I'm deep in thought,
perhaps about the way
the morning sun creates
crepuscular rays.

"Frankie!" he says,
with a nod of his head.

"Hey, Benjamin!" I say.
"I didn't know you lived here."

(Which is perfectly true,
except now I do,
I'm always coming this way.)

Benjamin has a sports bag
slung over his shoulder

and I don't know
what else to say,
so I ask,
"Have you got PE today?"

"Rugby trials," he says.
"Lunchtime."

"Cool," I say.
"Aren't you already
on the team?"

"Yeah," he says. "But
these are try-outs for the
first fifteen."

"What position
do you play?"

"Second row.
You're meant to be tall,
and strong as well.
I've got the height
but I need to work
on my upper back.
My lats, you know."

"No," I say.
"Which bit is that?"

"Here." He pats the muscles
beneath his armpits.
"I'm meant to be training.
Doing weights, you know?
Or, like, giving piggybacks.

If you need a ride…?"
He offers me his back,

     but

      I cannot reply.
My tongue is suddenly
too big for my mouth.

We walk a few steps
in silence,
and I wonder if he's
imagining the same
thing as me.

Me jumping on him,
our bodies touching
and me *riding him*.

   I glance at him and

Benjamin
is
blushing.

My cheeks go red
and I feel myself getting

                                    hot
                                    hot
                                    hot.

                            I look down,
                            searching for
                        something to say,
                        but Benjamin's legs
                        are in my eyes' way.
                    His school trousers *cling*
                    to his rugby-tight thighs,
                            and all at once
                                    I realize
                                the power
                    of a meaty pair of thighs.

                            I wonder what it
                                would be like
                                to bite them

                        and at the same time
                            I wonder what it
                                would be like
                                to tell Benjamin
                    this is what I'm thinking.

                            It's hard to imagine
                            doing something
                                so outrageous.

"I had so much fun
 on Saturday,"
he says. "I was hoping to

talk to you Monday,
or yesterday."

"Me too," I say.

"I really liked
hanging out with you."

I giggle, though
I don't mean to.

"Hey," he says, stopping
next to the park railings.
"Don't laugh at me.
I'm trying to say
I'm into you."

I stop too, though
it's hard not to move,
because suddenly
I'm full of rocket fuel.

"I like you too," I say
easily,
feeling my volatile
insides ignite.
"It was a shame
that night ended
when it did."

I take a step closer.

And Benjamin draws
        a little nearer to me
and whispers, "Do you think
it's too early?"

                                        "For what?" I ask,
                                        so close I can feel
                                        the biscuity-warmth
                                        of his breath on my face
                                        and realize that he's
                                                    talking
                                                    about
                                                    kissing.

        "For this," he says,
        then leans in,
        and brings his lips
        close to mine

                                            and I move my lips
                                                closer to his
                                            and just like that
                                                        we're

                    kissing
                by the railings
                in the golden
                    bright
                    morning
                    sunshine.

                    #Amazing

COLD SHOULDERS AND PIGGYBACKS

In *The Walking Dead*
the zombies are always
biting people's necks.
But as I leave Benjamin
at the school gate,
I glance again
at his rugby thighs
and realize if there is
an instinctive part
of the human brain
dedicated to eating
human flesh
it would definitely make
zombies bite the thighs.

They are,
undeniably,
the *meatiest* part
of the human body.

I stifle a snort
as I catch up with Marie,
and we walk into
physics class.
I wish Harriet were here.
Marie wouldn't get
why that's funny.

But then I realize
that Marie
hasn't actually said
a word to me.

I guess Harriet did
a thorough job
of turning her
against me.

I look around to catch
one more glimpse of
Benjamin, and instead
see Harriet get out of
her mum's bright yellow car
and walk through the gate,
head held high.

We file inside the physics lab
and Marie very deliberately
doesn't sit next to me.
She takes the last seat
on the row behind
where we usually sit
with Harriet.

Then the room comes alive
with whispers and murmurs
and a classroom of heads follows
as Harriet approaches.

She flicks her hair
theatrically for the benefit

of everyone watching.
I can't believe she's
enjoying this moment.
She looks totally fine.
Happy even.
I guess Mr Adamson
didn't call the police.

~~I wish he would.~~
~~She deserves it.~~

Harriet is heading towards
our classroom door but then
she struts right past,
and I watch through the window
as she goes into
the other class.

I guess Harriet got moved
so Mr B isn't teaching her.
I sit on my own.
I take out my phone
under the desk
just to check.

We're not allowed
phones in class,
we're meant to
leave them in our lockers.
Not that anyone bothers.

But Mr B won't be
expecting me

to break the rules.

I have a message from
Benjamin.
I open it,
smile at it.
Benjamin's message says:
Piggyback home?

I want to say yes because
all I can think of are
rugby-tight thighs.
Rugby-tight
ₜhighₛ.

My finger hovers on *reply*.
God, I want to …
bite his thighs.
How shall I reply?

But while I'm thinking
I'm not listening
to anything happening
in the room because
my mind is off with Benjamin.

Then Marie kicks
the back of my chair
and I look up to hear
Mr B say, "Ahem!"
in his particular way.

He scowls at me and taps the
box for confiscated phones.

I get up
and drop mine in,
blushing because I
usually wouldn't dare to
be
actually
messaging.

On my way back to my seat
I smile at Marie,
but she won't look at me.

MOMENTUM

"Open your books to page
one hundred and twelve,"
says Mr B. "Momentum."

I copy the equation
he's written on the board:
momentum = mass x velocity.

But then I start thinking,
if Benjamin gave me
a piggyback home,
how much more momentum
would we have
than if we were walking alone—
   "Frankie?" says Mr B.

         I look up.
       "Yes, sir?" I say
      with desperation,
        hoping he'll
     repeat the question.
  But he just points at the board
        and waits,
      and time ticks by
     as I try to calculate
  the answer to the equation.

"How about you, Marie?"
asks Mr B.

"Is it sixty?" she tries,
glancing at me.

But just in time,
I get there.
"Actually, it's sixty-nine,"
I say to the class
and everyone laughs.

(But Mr B doesn't like
that I can get the answer right
without even listening.)
(And neither does Marie.)

"Concentrate, Frankie,"
is all he says.

AFTER

I wait outside for Marie
with a dull ache
in my belly,
but she passes by
and blanks me.

"What's up with you?"
I ask.

She stops and gives me a filthy look,
like I'm scum of the earth.
"Er … Harriet?" she says,
like that's enough.

"What about her?"
I ask, wondering if
anything new
has happened
that I don't know.

"Wow. Really?
Frankie, she's meant to be,
like, your best mate.
And yesterday she had
the worst day,
and when she really needed you,
you were too busy judging
to listen to her."

I blink slowly.
So that's Harriet's story?
Nothing about her
trying to get me
into trouble?

"What happened with
Mr Adamson?" I ask.

"Ask her yourself."

"Marie!" I plead. "Just tell me.
I saw her this morning.
Did he call the police?"

Marie sighs, and faces me.
"She got detention,
like, every day
after school.
        And you
        didn't
        even
        message
        last night.
Don't you care
about her?"

"Of course I do."

"You've got a funny way
of showing it."

"I … I was…
I didn't know
what to say."

"Anything would have been
better than nothing."

"They didn't call
the police though.
That's good."

But Marie just
shakes her head
and walks off.

THE CHANGING ROOM

Harriet has successfully
spread the word
that we had a fight
and I'm the baddie.

At lunch I grab a baguette
and eat it behind the trees,
where I can see
the boys doing rugby.

I watch Benjamin('s thighs)
and compose my reply
to his question
about carrying me home.

I try to write something sexy,
but that's Harriet's style,
so in the end
I just put **OK**.

Immediately after trials,
he replies to me, saying,
Great! Meet you at the gate.
I go to PE, feeling
(for the first time
since mine and Harriet's fight)
happy.

In the changing room
Harriet and the girls ignore me.
Instead they
comb over and over
Harriet's drama
and how shit it is
that everyone is sharing
the photo Jackson took of it.
It's the talk of the school.
We all know there'll be
something new tomorrow.

But anyway, I don't want to speak.
I'm too excited, wondering
whether Benjamin might
actually try to carry me.

So I just put on my leggings,
T-shirt and trainers
in silence, with my
inappropriate thoughts
safely sealed behind my lips.

"Whatever
you're smiling about,"
Harriet says, pushing past me,
"I'm not asking,
so get out of my face."

> I didn't even know
> I was smiling.

This thing between
Benjamin and me
is making me feel giddy.

It's like air.
You can't see it,
but it's comprised
of a myriad of
infinitesimally
small particles
of unimaginable
complexity and beauty.

Not even Harriet
being snarky
bothers me.

In the gym
we form a circle
for warm-up,
Harriet opposite me,
scowling.

And when we play basketball,
I go on the opposite team
to mark Harriet.
I'm so bouncy,
I absolutely kill it.

AFTER GYM

After gym
I'm sticky
and sweating.

I sniff myself.
I stink and
I'm walking home
with Benjamin.

Hardly anyone ever
has a shower
(they're open-plan)
but I decide to do it anyway.

I strip and grab a towel
and with as much dignity
as I can, say,
"I need a shower today,
so look away."

And to my amazement,
Leylah, Marie, Bethany
and the others
do what I say.

And I realize that I *can* be
pretty brave.

CHANGING-ROOM TALK

While I'm in the shower,
Harriet says, "Wow, she's *brave*."

And Leylah says, "Yeah.
I would never
have a shower in school."

Then Bethany says,
"Me neither. For a start I can't
wash my hair, cos of the dye.
But anyway, I hate these bits,
and these bits here."

Leylah says, "You've got
a beautiful body, Beth."

And Bethany says,
"Aw, thanks, babe."

"You're so gay, Leylah,"
Harriet chips in.

"And?" says Leylah.

"All right, Ley.
Keep your tits on,"
Harriet replies.
"Anyway, I meant Frankie is
brave sending Mr B

this picture of herself…"
She holds up my phone.

I hear the sound
of a message sending

and I'm already running,
slipping on wet tiles
as I hear Marie shout,

"HARRY! YOU
DID
        NOT
                SEND
                    THAT?!"

BETRAYAL

I grab
my phone
out of her hand.

Harriet has taken
a picture of me.
In the shower.
Naked.

"Tell me you have not
sent this to Mr B," I gasp,
frantically swiping
to find my sent items.
I can feel tears coming.

"Calm down," Harriet says.
"Of course I haven't.
I only sent it to the girls.
I'm just having a laugh.
Lighten up, won't you?"

The girls get out their phones
and Bethany says,
"We'll all delete it,
won't we?"

Leylah nods and looks shocked.
"It's gone," she says.

"Jesus, Harriet,"
Marie says.
"Get some bloody
boundaries."

                                    I delete it,
                              then shove my phone
                           back in the front pocket
                                        of my bag.

"Calm down," says Harriet.
"I'm just
joking."

                              As I return to the shower
                                      I feel her eyes
                                 like a knife in my back.

REVENGE

I turn off the tap.
            Dry myself.
                        Pull on my uniform.
                                    Take deep breaths.

There is total silence.
No one knows
what to say.

And I know
it's a low blow
but I really want to
get Harriet back.

My mind goes to the
Silent Ladies' Agreement
to NOT bring up how
in primary school,
year two,
Harriet pooed
in the middle of assembly.
She's crossed a line.
I will too.

                        I shake out my wet hair,
                    then pause in front of her.
                                "See ya later,
                                Harriet Plopper."

The others gasp,
but they also laugh.
And that's good enough
for me.

I leave the changing room,
stepping outside,
my still-damp skin
tingling in the wind,

feeling
like
a warrior,

to meet Benjamin.

NIGHTCLUB THIGHS

On my way across the playground,
Mrs Lovelie, who takes PSHE
(and is not at all lovely),
shouts across the yard at me.

"Frankie Young!
Roll your skirt down!
You're in a school playground,
not on a nightclub podium!"

Then she walks out of the gate,
right past Benjamin,
who is wearing
tiny
little
rugby shorts
over his
rugby-tight thighs.

His are the legs
that should be
on a podium.

BIOLOGY

Benjamin is leaning
against the school wall.
I watch his shoulders rise and f$_{all}$
as though the air inside him
is riding him
from within.

The late spring wind
sweeps the clouds aside
and in the sudden sun
his white rugby top glows bright.
I blink against his blinding light.

I step a little closer,
my arm muscles stiffening
with a nervously tense,
trembly feeling
as I tap his shoulder.
He's waiting for me
and
        oh my life,
                I can't NOT see his thighs.

Benjamin turns and gives me
a grin with dimples
– a thing of beauty,
a gift from the gods –

and I find my mind
s
l
i
p
s
to the word

bite.

God, I want to
bite his thighs.

"Hop on," he says
with a nod to his back.

I want to ride him
all the way home
but I'm not sure
if it's rude,
considering what I'm thinking
is not what he's offering.

"No, really, it's fine," I say.

"OK," says Benjamin,
with a shrug of his shoulders,

which makes
the blood rush
to my cheeks

and down below
I feel a tingle.

"Can I still walk you
home?" he asks.

                                        I nod,
                        my heart in my mouth,
                        my mind in my pants.

As we leave,
I see Harriet
through the window.
She's sitting in the corridor
outside the head's office.
She looks worried,
and I feel guilty,
which is annoying
because her drama
is nothing to do with me.

                                Or not any more
                                        anyway.
                        She made it that way.

THE SPACE BETWEEN US

On the way home,
    the space between
        Benjamin and me
           seems to shrink
        as we chat
          until gradually
            our shoulders are bumping.

"Have you seen that photo?"
he asks,

          and I think for a moment
        he means the naked one of me,
        then I wonder if he means
        the picture from Harriet
          to Mr B.

But then he adds,
"Of the black hole?"

    And I'm so relieved.
    It's cool he's into
    the same stuff as me.
    Talking to him is so easy.

          I nod.
        "It blows my mind.
        Do you ever think
        how we're so lucky?
        Like, witnessing
        so many things that

the human eye
has never seen before.
We're living through history."

"I've never thought about it
like that," he says.
"You're right.
It's so easy
to take for granted
all the amazing things
we've seen
because of photography."

And briefly,
I think about Harriet
and the things people have seen
because of her photography.

EVERYTHING ABOUT HIM

I like how
when Benjamin talks
his voice goes soft,
like he's singing.

I like how
when he walks
his curly hair bounces,
like he's on the
sprung floor
of the gymnasium.

I like how
even though they're mates,
he knows
Jackson hasn't grown up
at all since primary school.

I like how
he asks what I think about things
that are actually interesting.

I like how
as we walk home
his ideas seem to change
and wrap around mine
so that what we are saying
seems to be creating
some kind of new meaning

in the shrinking space
between us.

I like how
he stops beside
the railings of the park again
to kiss me,
just like this morning.

I like
where this is going.

I like everything about him.

FINGERS

As we near my house,
I find
that my mind
wanders from

our conversation
so I'm not
thinking about
anything much

because all
I want to do
is touch
Benjamin

and it's strangely
peaceful to find
my mind
is mostly
in my fingers.

HOW DO YOU GET *THERE?*

We reach my house.
There's no one home,
and in the doorway
Benjamin stands
teetering on the threshold
with his dimpled grin
and his shoulders
rising and falling.

> I want to
> grab him
> and pull him in.

Our mouths say goodbye
but our bodies linger
because
(I think)
our fingers
have other ideas.

> "Do you want to come in?
> There's nobody home."

He shrugs. "OK."
And just like that
he steps in.

He puts down his bag
and takes off his trainers.

He's not wearing socks
so it's weird for a second
because Benjamin's
naked feet
are touching my carpet.

I've seen bare feet
a million times before,
but now they seem
completely obscene.

I stare at his feet
and start to feel hot
so I take off my shoes
and I take off my socks
and I take off my tie.
And my shirt falls open
and Benjamin's eyes
fall on my bra.

"Are you thirsty?" I ask.

Benjamin nods
and swallows so loudly
I actually hear it.

I go to the kitchen
but all I'm thinking is:
how do we get from
here
                    to
                                    there?

Back in the hall,
I hand him a glass and
as it passes between us
it slips through our fingers
so blackcurrant squash
splatters our tops
and stains the carpet.

"Shit," exclaims Benjamin.

                                        "Shit," I echo.

Then we both look down
at our wet tops
(and if his shorts
were clinging before,
now they are wet-look Lycra).

"This is my only rugby top.
I should give it a wash."

                              "Then you should take it off,"
                                    I say, giggling a little
                                    at the words coming
                                        out of my mouth.

"We both should,"
he says, lifting his top
over his head.

                                          "OK." I laugh.
                              My heart beats so hard
                              beneath my stained shirt

that I can see my skin trembling
as I undo the buttons.

"Should we go to your room?"
he says, looking around.

I shake my head.
I don't want to move,
to break the moment.
"My parents won't be
home for ages."

Then we look at each other,
still smiling from laughing
but now we're both blushing.

I think we both know
we're about to go

there.

And just like Harriet
said it would be,
as we press
our hot chests
skin to skin,
body to body,
I find that I can
just be me.

Then our lips touch,
and we're kissing
with tongues

and the breath from our lungs
mingles together and
enters the other.

This is so much more fun
than I thought it would be.

"I WANT TO BITE YOUR THIGHS"

I murmur.

Oh my God.

Did I *say* that?
Can I say that?
Can I even *think* that?

But
"OK,"
Benjamin says.
Then, "This is fun."

HIS THIGHS

From a distance,
Benjamin's thighs are statuesque,
the thighs of Michelangelo's *David*,
sculpted perfection.

Yet now I feel them,
they're bulge and flex,
heat and sweat,
as I
    press my cheeks
      against his flesh
    and lick his skin,
which tastes
of him.

I touch my teeth to him,
    and
      bite
    his
thighs.

GIGGLING

"Wow," I say, giggling
as my whole body takes in
the hot wetness of his
bare chest skin.

"Shit," says Benjamin,
giggling. "Are we allowed
to do this on a school day?"

                              "I'm OK with it
                          if you're OK," I say,
                                      giggling.

Benjamin nods,
smiling.
"I'm definitely OK."

            I like this about him.
            Despite the intensity
        of what our hands are doing,
            we're both still giggling.

FUN

I expected my first time
getting serious like this
to be *so* serious.
But it's *so* not.

In fact Benjamin and I are
still laughing,
gasping at the fun of
using nothing but our hands
and fingers
and our joined solar plexuses
to make each other come.

CRIME SCENE

We lie on the floor
of the hall
of my house,
panting
and laughing.

A smashed vase
and broken glass
and our discarded tops
decorate the wet carpet.

"That *was* fun,"
Benjamin says.

> "It was," I agree,
> sitting up slightly
> and gazing around.
> "It looks like a crime scene."

Benjamin props himself up too,
and looks at the mess
of flowers and clothes,
laughing,

then,

> at the same moment,
> we both glance down

at Benjamin's hands
and see blood
on his fingers.

"Shit!" he says, getting up,
turning his hands over,
searching for a cut.

My stomach drops.
I touch the tips of my fingers
to my knickers
and from the sticky feeling
know what's happened.

I cringe
and shrink
and desperately try and try to think
of a way to make this
situation go away.

Benjamin looks terrified.
"I don't think I'm bleeding,"
he says.
"Are you OK?"

"Yes," I say,
dying inside.
"I'm OK. I've just …
come on."
I scrunch up my face.

Benjamin's silent
and I glance at him,

and he looks
at me
blankly.

Oh my God.
I'm going to have to
explain this frankly.
"You know,
I came *on*...
I got my period.
It's menstrual blood."

WHY did my first time
saying *menstrual blood*
outside of biology
have to also be
the first time
anything remotely sexy
has ever happened to me?

"Oh!" he says slowly,
looking between his bloody
fingers and me.
"I see."

IT'S ONLY BLOOD

Benjamin doesn't move
and he doesn't look at me.
"Are you OK?" he asks.
"Did I … hurt you?"

> "No," I say,
> shaking my head.
> "It was … good."

"Are you sure?" he says,
still looking down at his fingers.

> I don't know
> whether he's talking
> about hurting me
> or satisfying me.
> This is so embarrassing.
> "I'm really OK," I say.
> "It's just my period."

"Phew," he sighs, nodding
like he's trying to catch up.
"I guess it's only blood."

> "Yeah," I agree.
> "Totally. Only blood."
>
> I know it is only blood,
> but no one else
> usually sees your period.

"Ugh," I groan. "I'm cringing."

"It's fine," he says,
though it feels like he's
trying to convince himself
as much as me.
"I've got a sister,
remember?"
Then he sniggers.
"Which in this context
makes me sound
like a massive weirdo."

I laugh nervously.
"It's OK. I know
what you mean."

"Phew." He grins.
"I just mean …
I know about periods and stuff.
I don't mind blood.
It's biology.
I'm actually thinking
about doing medicine
at university."
He finally looks up at me,
grinning widely.

"Massive weirdo alert,"
I say, grinning back.

Benjamin laughs
and then we're both

giggling, when suddenly
the letter box clatters
and we both jump up,
scrambling from the floor,
diving for cover,

as nothing more
than a newspaper
lands in the hall.

We look from the paper,
to one another.

                                    I've managed to grab
                         my dad's high-vis cycling vest
                                         to cover myself,
                                    even though I'm only
                                         half undressed.

But Benjamin has got
a Kim Kardashian selfie book,
with a massive picture of
her face and boobs,
over his crotch,
covering the wet patch
on his pants.

                                         I snort as he

looks down
to see what he's holding.

"Ergh!" he says. "Why do you
have this?!"

I cover my mouth,
laughing at the sight of him.
"Harriet gave it to me
for my birthday.
She thought I'd like it,
because it's about
photography,
but I think she actually
wanted it for herself."

"Now I really need
to wash my hands," he says.

"The bathroom's up there."

He backs up the stairs,
with Kim Kardashian's face
still held in place.
"I didn't know you were
into photography."

"I'm not," I say. "Harriet is.
But we do take photos
of the moon and stars together.
I'm maybe more of the astronomer
and Harriet's the photographer.
But we both love both.
I'll show you if you like."

AFTERNOON STARGAZING

We sit cross-legged
on my bedroom carpet,
his rugby shirt
under my hairdryer,
me fully dressed,
him wearing only a towel.

"This is a bit unfair,"
Benjamin says,
over the warmth
of the electric whirr.

He waves the hairdryer
at his shirt,

                        which I'm holding.
                           It is billowing,
            rippling over my fingers,
releasing the smell of him.
         I want to kiss him again.

                         I show him mine
              and Harriet's pictures
                of the night sky,
         collected on the account
            she made where we post
            anything good we take.

"They're amazing," he says.
"When do you do it?"

"Whenever it's dark.
Sometimes we have sleepovers,
then get pastries
from the bakery
on the high street.
It opens at, like, 2 a.m."

"You get up that early?"

"Hell, no," I say.
"We stay awake that late!"

"Just doing astronomy?"

I laugh. "Actually,
mostly talking."

"What do you talk about?"

"Everything."
It used to be true.

"Everything?"

I nod. "Pretty much."

I wish we weren't
in this stupid fight.
Tonight, when Benjamin's gone,
who am I going to tell
about this seminal boy thing?

"What about you?
Who do you talk to?
Jackson?"

"No way," he scoffs.
"We've been mates
for ever, but I don't tell him
anything.
I'm close to my sister.
But she's in California now.
She's a programmer."

"California must be nice."

"Yeah, for her," he says.
"I really miss her."

Benjamin looks around my room,
then says, "Nice curtains,"
nodding towards the window
and laughing again.

I look at my curtains
that I've had
since I was seven.
The illustrated stars,
planets and rockets
so familiar
I almost don't see them.

I read the exclamations
scattered all over them,

like *"Totally Cosmic!"*
"Blast Off!" and
"Intergalactic!"

"Yeah," I say. "I was a bit
obsessed with space."

"And you took
all those photos
you just showed me
because you're over it?"

"OK," I say. "I'm still obsessed.
Anyway, I'm allowed to express
myself in my own room."

"I said they're *nice*."
He grins. "In fact, they're
totally cosmic."

"Your top is ready."

He turns off the hairdryer,

and I quickly sniff
his warm-shirt smell
before handing it back.

"So how does your space
obsession manifest
these days?" he asks,
pulling his top over his curly hair.
"Other than taking pictures."

"I'll show you."

We lie beneath the skylight
and I open an app on my phone
that lets you stargaze
(or as close as you can to it)
in broad daylight.

I hold my phone,
heavy and cool in my hot hand,
panning across constellations,
then point to the waxing
gibbous moon.
"It's on its way to being full."

"How do you know?"

"Well…" I hesitate,
wondering how nerdy to be.
"In the northern hemisphere,
a waxing moon is illuminated
on the right."

"That's very cool.
So when will it be full?"

"Next week.
There's actually a lunar eclipse
on Wednesday,
which means there'll be
a blood moon.
It'll be amazing."

"Cool," he says. "Could I see
the moon one night? Like,
through your telescope?"

"Sure. We always go up
on a full moon.
Unless it's cloudy,
or the timing isn't right."

"But you can see the stars
any night, as long as it's clear?"

"Yep." I nod.
"Weather permitting.
But they're always there.
They're there now, you know.
We don't think about it
because the sun is so bright,
but we're also
bathing in starlight."

"That is … intergalactic!"
He grins, but I know
he's not being sarcastic.
He actually means it.

EYE GAZING

We gaze at the stars
        a bit,
but actually,
        it's more interesting
                gazing at each other.

I didn't think there could be
any singular thing
more interesting than
the whole of the rest
of the universe.

Benjamin leans closer to me,
narrows his eyes and says,
"I can actually see
the strands of muscle
that make up the front
pigmented fibrovascular layer
of your iris."

                        "Wow," I say, my crush
                        on Benjamin extending.
                "I didn't think this was possible,
                        but are you an even bigger
                                nerd than me?"

"No way," he says,
 pointing over at the window.
"Exhibit A: curtains."

CHICKEN THIGHS

Most nights Dad cooks
while I talk about my day
until Mum gets home,
but tonight I stay in my room,
waiting until I absolutely have to
go to the kitchen.

Just before seven,
Dad calls me.
"Frankie! Dinner is served!"

Mum puts her laptop bag down
and comes over to kiss me,
before sitting down opposite.

"How was school?" she asks
            from far away
            across the table
            and the galaxy.

"Yes!" says Dad.
"Tell us everything."

                              I am silent.
                      I can hardly tell them
                  "I walked home with a boy"
                                          or
                        "I got my period on him"
                                          and

I definitely cannot risk
letting slip
"I bit
that boy
(on his rugby-tight thighs)
(in our hallway)
(naked)
(and spilled blackcurrant squash)
(and had an orgasm)
(that's when I got my period)
(on his fingers)."

So I just say,
"Good, thanks."

"Did Mr B read your application?"
Mum asks, pushing her glasses up
her nose with one finger.

"I've just sent it," I say.
"He said he'll give me
my reference on Friday."

"Excellent!" Dad smacks
me on the back.
"Hairy's applying too,
isn't she?"

I don't want to talk
about Harriet,
so I just nod.

"We are so proud of you,"
Mum says.

"I know," I say
and try not to think about
what I really did today
as I bite
into Dad's famous
barbecued chicken thighs.

A PICTURE

I'm in bed at 10 p.m.
when my phone goes *ting*.
I sweep it up, caressing it.
I know it's him.

Benjamin
Thinking bout you.

Me
Me too.

Benjamin
Send me a pic?

And those four little words
make my insides
go squish.

Benjamin
with godlike thighs,
a delicious grin
and naked feet
inside his shoes
and clever thoughts
inside his head

wants a picture
of me.

SELFIE

I take a few.
I look all right,
but then the questions start
  like:

How much skin?
Pyjamas in?
Straps or skin?

Lying down
or sitting up
or not in bed?

I think
about Benjamin.

I licked his skin,
I bit him,
I menstruated on him.

He said, "It's only blood,"
and laughed at my curtains
and loved my pictures of the moon.

Then I remember
the picture Harriet
took of me
under the trees
after things started

happening with Benjamin and me
at the ice rink that night.

I find it
and that's the one
I send him.

Straight away, it says,

Benjamin is typing...

Benjamin
You are so pretty.
Here's one of me.
Just for you.
Night x

He's in bed,
smiling,
with bare shoulders.
I can't get enough of it.
I stare and stare and stare
at it, until my eyes are tired

and I sigh
and lie back
on my bed,
my phone pressed
against my chest,
the weight of it
pinning me to this
perfect moment.

PART
TWO

THE FUNDAMENTALS OF PHYSICS

Harriet steps out of her front door
at the exact same moment as me
and I imagine on another day
telling her about Benjamin
and what we did,
and the pictures we swapped
late at night in bed,
but instead she raises
her middle finger at me
and says, "Bitch."

"Takes one to know
one," I say and turn
the other way.
She's the one
who took a photo of me
in the shower at school.
Talk about bitchy.

I don't need her anyway.
She said I'm nothing to her.
Well, she can be nothing to me.

I walk to school with
the wind in my hair,
the morning sun
glistening on the dew.

I feel #NoFilter fit.
I'm textbook.
I've totally got it.

On his street
Benjamin is waiting for me,
leaning against the brick wall
outside his house.
He stands,
and crosses to meet me.

                      "Good morning," I say.
                        "Nice to see you."

"Hey, you," he replies,
 smiling and walking beside me.
"Sleep OK?"

                          "I did," I say.
                          "You?"

"Well," he says,
 our feet in sync.
"I had this
 weird dream that you and me
 were in space."

                  "Like astronauts?" I say,
                  glancing at him sideways.

"Actually, we weren't
 exactly in space,

we were swimming around
like there was no gravity."

"With spacesuits on?"

"Nope."

"So we were dead."

Benjamin laughs.
"We were
sort of in a drawing…"
He hesitates.
"Like your curtains."

I laugh, nudging him.
"You dreamed
about my curtains!"

"Well, they are
totally cosmic!"

*"You dreamed about
my curtains,"* I crow,
loving the feeling

of *my things*
making it into
his subconscious.

"Did you dream
about me?"
Benjamin asks,

and I wish I could lie,
but I hardly ever
remember my dreams.
"I thought about you.
A lot," I say.

Then Benjamin leans in,
with this sweet uncertainty,
and very lightly kisses me.

I kiss him back,
and feel a rush
of blood to my head
at us kissing
so casually,
so comfortably,
so familiarly.

L i f e   i s   a m a z i n g.

Our lips come apart,
and that's when I get
the ooze-squish-blob
of falling blood:
impending f
            l
             o
              o
               d.

(How the frick did my
ultra-plus tampon
fill up so quick?)

Benjamin takes my hand
and we start to walk,
our swinging arms
bumping lightly
                but

                          I'm walking funny.
                          I cannot let my pants
                                and tights meet,
                          because once they do,
                               the blood will find
                                        a path.

                               Then
                                  I
                               will
                                 be
                           done for.
                    That's fluid dynamics.

                    (The period woman
                who came in year six said,
                        "It's only blood,
                    just an egg-cupful,
            nothing to be embarrassed about."
                But when did she last try to
                    pull with an egg-cupful
                       of blood in her pants?)

"You're limping,"
says Benjamin.
"You OK?"

                          "I pulled my … thigh,"
                          I say with #InstantBlush.

The first word that came to mind.
(Obviously.)

We take one step.
His arm s l i d e s under mine.
"Here, you can lean on me."

My heart goes squish.
Then with one wrong step
my pants and tights meet.

I walk beside Benjamin,
our bodies touching,
knowing I now have
wet and sticky

thighs.

"What?" says Benjamin.

"What?" I say.

"You said *thighs.*"

"I don't think I did."

"You definitely did."

But I don't want to bring up
my period,
after what we did.
So I limp on.

"I can give you a piggyback,"
he offers. "It would help
with my training."

But I just shake my head
and say, "No thanks,"
hoping I can keep my secret
in my pants.

At the school gate,
Benjamin looks around,
then very quickly
pecks me
on the cheek.
"See you later?"

"Sure," I say,
tingling where the tickly
feeling of his kiss
on my cheek
briefly distracts me
from the creeping,
crampy feeling
in my womb.

Then I hurry away,
calculating how long
it will take
to get to the toilets
and change my tampon
and get back to class.
#Embarrassing

RUMOURS

I'm only a minute late
to history. Ms Wyse
is running late,
and from the tone
of the pre-lesson murmur
there's definitely
         something
                  happening
and I wonder
if Harriet's selfie
sent to Mr B
is still going strong.
It could last the week,
or maybe make the leap
to other schools
and go on and on.

Benjamin's at the back
with the boys.
He avoids my gaze
as I sit beside Marie,
who has stopped ignoring me
since Harriet took that photo
of me in the shower.

Then
   I
            hear
      one
               word
   above
            the
   white
         noise
      of
            gossiping.

P e r i o d .

I whip my head round
to look at Benjamin.

I stare at him.
He must be able to tell
I'm looking at him,
but he will not
look at me.
He hides his face
behind his history book.

I check my phone,
but there's nothing.
Bethany leans in to Leylah
and Marie,
glancing at me,
unsure if she's allowed
to talk to me.

"Gossip!" she says,
   then cups her hand
    whispering,
      gradually more quietly.
        "Jackson just told me
          Benjamin
           fingered someone
             on their period!"

"Ergh!" Leylah bursts out.
"That's DISGUSTING."

                The damp patch in my pants
                  is pressing coldly
                  against my skin,
                  and I'm sweating.

                I watch Marie
          as her face bunches up
                  in disgust
                  at the gossip.

                  About me.

                  And I swallow
                  the acid feeling
                  creeping up my throat.

Benjamin told *Jackson*
what we did?

I try to imagine Benjamin,
just now,

after he kissed me,
b r a g g i n g
to Jackson and the boys
about getting off with me,
about touching me,
about fingering me.

The betrayal freezes me,
physically.
I turn again, jerkily,
to try to make Benjamin
look
at
me.

But he won't.

Bethany's saying,
"That's so grim!"

And Marie asks the others,
"What do you think of him?"

"He's fit," says Leylah.

"I wonder if he's free,"
says Bethany.

Then Harriet looks at me slyly,
and says, "He fancies you,
doesn't he, Frankie?"

She's too close to the truth.
"I think I preferred it
when you weren't
talking to me."

"Someone's got PMT,"
she says, making
the others snigger.

None of them consider
it could actually have been me.

The one thing I have
at the moment
is that no one
seems
to know
it was me.

Still, I can't stop imagining
all the boys this morning,
laughing as Benjamin
made our intimacy
something funny.

The thing is, it was funny.
But it was funny between us.

BREAK TIME

It's all anyone talks about
in the queue at break,
because everyone revels in
the opportunity to be
disgusted by something.

"It's revolting!" Leylah says.

"I bet it went
e v e r y w h e r e!"
Harriet says,
nibbling her flake,
then making a face
like she's going to faint
(which she actually did
in year eight
when we dissected a frog
and she saw blood).

"Can we drop it now?"
Marie asks,
unwrapping a flapjack.
"Some of us are about to eat."

Harriet gives Leylah a look,
which points the finger
at Marie.

"Who would do
something like that?"
Harriet asks,
and I notice
her glancing over
at Jackson,
who is probably
asking his mates
the same thing.

Harriet looks at me.
"Come on, Frankie,
tell us what you think."

                                    I want to say,
                                    "It's only blood,"
                        but that would be as good
                                    as a confession,
                                        so I say,
                            "I thought you weren't
                                    talking to me?"

She gives me
a filthy look,
and says,
"Why are you standing
near me then?"

                                    "I must have
                                        forgotten
                                        how much I
                                        dislike you,"
                                I say, shrugging,
                                        then I leave

to search the crowd
in the concrete playground
for Benjamin,

to ask him
why he blabbed
our secret.

POPULARITY

At the end of break,
I spot him
right before we go in
to sex and relationships education.

He stares at me
like a wild animal
caught in the open
and I want to hurt him.

I go to the corner
of the building and
beckon him with my head
to follow me.

I fight the urge to
SHOUT AT HIM.
"You told Jackson?"

"I didn't! I swear."

"Well, you told someone!
Or how does the
whole school know?"

"I hoped it was you."

"Me?" I say,
looking at his panicked face.

"Why would *I* tell *anyone*?"

"Not even Harriet?
You said you tell
her everything."

"We're not talking."

"Shit," he says,
flattening his curly hair
beneath his interlaced fingers.
He has a circle of sweat
in each armpit.

"Did you tell the boys
you were with me?" I ask.

But he just breathes out,
head back,
looking at the sky.

"Benjamin!
What did you tell them?"

"There he is!" Jackson yells,
striding around the corner.
"Up top! You dawg."

I want to melt into nothing,
become invisible,
try to not be standing here
in broad daylight
with Benjamin,

who
scowls
at Jackson,
leaving him
      hanging.

      (The first decent thing
      he's done
      all morning.)

"Come on, Benji.
Tell us who you fing—"

           "Get lost, Jackson,"
           Benjamin says,
           glancing briefly
           at me.
      But that makes
      Jackson notice me.

                 There's nowhere to hide.

"Not her?" he scoffs,
looking me over dismissively.
"Harriet told me she's frigid.
Come on, who was it?
Does she go to our school?"

Benjamin stands up
a little straighter.
"I said get lost, Jackson."
He laughs lightly.

"I'll see you in class,
you massive twat."

Jackson looks me up
and down
one more time,
then leaves

                                    me feeling
                                like I've been
                            slapped in the face.

            Harriet told Jackson I'm *frigid*?
            What else did she tell him?

                                    I stand there,
                                feeling lonely,
                                    thinking
                        I can't trust anybody.

"At least no one knows
it was you," he hisses.
"*Everyone* is talking about me."

                                    This is true.
                                    Everyone *is*
                            talking about him.
                        But it's not embarrassing.

                                    "Yeah," I say,
                            realizing something.
                        "And you've never been
                                more popular."

THE HUNT

Later, in the lunch hall,
I hear Jackson's voice,
loud above
the clatter of cutlery
and chatter of the crowd.

"Come on, girls.
Who is on?"
he howls,
a bloodhound
with a scent.

The girls all scream
with shrill denial.
      "Oh my God!"
            "Not me!"
      "Nor me!"
              "I'm not due for ages."
        "It's disgusting."

But not one of them says,

"It's only blood."

           It is only blood.
                  Only blood.

                     But nor do I.

I just eat my chips
at an empty table,
wishing I had a
packed lunch today.

Harriet doesn't
bother me.
She's too busy
asking everyone
who they think
this mystery girl might be,

making sure
the gossip stays on this
juicy new topic,
and doesn't come back to her
and her ridiculous selfie.

On my way to the toilets
before the last class,
there's a crowd
gathered outside
the girls' loos,
which is so annoying
because I need to
change my tampon.

Clutching a new one
in my pocket,
I try to sidle through,
but in the middle of it all,
I end up next to Benjamin.

"Frankie!" he hisses
into my ear. "You should
get out of h—"

"WRITE YOUR NAME
HERE IF YOU'RE ON!"
a voice shouts.
Jackson.

He's sticking a piece of paper
to the toilet door.
"Come on, ladies," he shouts.
"Own up. Who's riding
the crimson wave?"

He scans the crowd
then stops on Harriet.
"What about you?" he says.
"Everyone knows you're
dirty, you prick-tease."

Harriet scoffs at him.
"I thought I wasn't your type
anyway. We're not family."

"What's that supposed to mean?"
Jackson throws back.

"Those girls from your threesome?
That photo you showed us
with them kissing your cheeks?
They're your cousins, right?"

A few people titter
and Jackson looks furious,

and I think he's really
about to go for her,
but then she

turns around
and surveys the crowd
like she's the queen and
judge of everything
and says, "Maybe it was Marie.
She's always had a heavy flow."

I gasp.

I know Harriet is
sometimes mean
but I cannot believe she
is directing her cruelty at Marie.

(Marie got her period first
and all us girls know
it's heavy,
but for Harriet
to break Marie's privacy,
to tell *everybody*,
is almost beyond belief.)

Harriet did think
it was funny to send
a sexy selfie to Mr B
and to take a photo of me
in the shower.

"Harriet!" I say
as I shake my head.

"What?" She shrugs,
pretending she doesn't know
what she's done.
She should just say sorry.

I take a step back
and catch my heel on
Benjamin's bag
and stumble back,
        my hands flailing,
                my tampon skittering,
                        rolling and stopping
                                at the toilet door.
                                        I land on the floor.

Harriet gasps then
        sees my face,
        sees Benjamin,
both of us blushing.

She raises an eyebrow
as she looks at
him,
        eyes narrowing.

"Frankie," she says,
her face changing.

The crowd falls silent.

                                        "Leave it, Harry."

"It wasn't her,"
 she says to Jackson quickly.

"She's practically a *nun*,"
 she tells everyone, laughing.
"Do nuns even have periods?"

                            "Why are you helping him?"
                            I ask, nodding to Jackson.

"Bitch fight!" Jackson cries,
 but no one joins in.
 Everyone is looking
 between me
 and Harriet.

Marie goes up
 to the toilet door
 and picks up the tampon
 from the floor,
 then with one swift tug
 tears down the paper.

"Oi!" says Jackson.
"Who said you could do that?"

"Statistically," says Marie,
 facing Jackson,
"about a quarter of
 menstruating women

are on at any one time,
so this" – she waves the paper –
          "is bullshit.

          And anyway,
          do you know how boring it is
          what you're doing?
          Periods are normal.
          You're the weird thing."

Then she scrunches it up
and throws it
at the bin next to me.
"Everyone ignore him."

"It was Marie!"
Jackson hollers.
"Benjamin fingered
slutty little Marie
when she was
on the blob!"

                              I feel guilty,
                              and relieved
                                  she's taken
                              the heat off me,
                          because my cheeks
                              are threatening
                              to give me away.

Marie looks angry
but Jackson is still going.

"I can smell your fanny
from here, Marie.
Blood and…"
  He sniffs the air.
            "Cum."

There are a few laughs,
and briefly
I see Marie's mask falter.
Not anger …
perhaps humiliation?
Or regret for sticking
        out her neck.

No one is saying anything.
Not even Harriet.
She's just letting Marie get it.

                      I pick myself up
                            and say,
            "As if you'd know what
              a fanny smells like."

Jackson swings around
to look at me.
"The nun said *fanny*!"

              "Shut up, Jackson.
      The closest you've ever been
      to the inside of a girl's pants
          is right where you are now.
    Lurking outside the girls' toilets."

Then everyone
laughs
at him,

because of me.

"I've just remembered,"
Jackson says,
regaining the crowd.
"I did see Benjamin
with someone earlier.
What were you two
whispering about,
Freaky Frankie?"

"We weren't whispering,"
Benjamin says quickly.

Far.
Too.
Quickly.

The colour of my cheeks
is all Jackson needs.
I swallow
loudly.

"It *WAS* Frankie!"
Jackson screams.
"You.

Dirty.

Sluuuuuuuut!"

For a moment
I stand still.
I can survive this.
If I don't move,
Jackson will back down.
But then

everyone turns around
to look at me
and in the crowd I see
Leylah and Bethany
and on their faces
I catch a flicker of
something.

Disgust?

Do they think
I'm disgusting?

I am breaking.
I don't even stop
to pick up my bag.

I run
crying,
crumbling.
I am disgusting.

HARRIET'S ADVICE

In the other loos,
I pull my feet up,
crouching on the lidless seat,
my f i n g e r s clinging
to the **crusty** rim.
There's no point worrying
about what I'm touching.
I am the dirty thing.

"Frankie!" a voice snaps at me
impatiently as a door bangs closed
and angry footsteps approach.

Harriet's hair drapes on the floor
as her face peeps
under the cubicle door.

She stands and sighs.
"Mr Guerra made me
come get you.
He knows you're in.
If you don't come now,
he's going to mark you
down as truant."

                              "I don't care," I say,
                              trying not to sniff.

"You can't hide in here all afternoon,"
Harriet says. "Don't make
it *worse* than it needs to be."

                              "Harriet,
                         you have no idea
                    what you're talking about
                           so just get lost."

"Come on, Frankie.
Don't be so weak.
You'll get through this.
I did."

                              "It's not the same."

"It's not *that* different."

                         "It is! What's happening
                              to me is worse."

"Worse than getting moved
into the thick class?
Worse than a teacher
telling on you because
he thought you were
trying to pull him?"

                              (Which she was.)

"And everyone seeing
the picture that was sent?"

I can't believe she thinks
she's the victim.
She sent it.

"Toughen up.
Just tell everyone
to grow up."

"I just got called a slut.
For nothing."

"Well…" she says, pausing.
She's loving this.
"Not *nothing*.
You did let Benjamin
finger you
on your period.
You're not even going
out with him!"

"What the hell, Harriet?
Since when were you
the judge of what's decent?"

"I'm just saying.
It wasn't *nothing*."

"You *sexted* a teacher,"
I shout through the door.
"That's so much worse."

"But much less slutty."

"You told Jackson
that I'm *FRIGID*."

"Well, you proved me wrong,
didn't you?"

"Just leave me alone."

"I'd love to.
I'll let Mr Guerra know
you'll be crying in here
all afternoon over nothing."

"If you only came here
to tell me my problems
are nothing, you've done that."

"I came here to tell you
you're making a mistake
hiding away
like you've done something
to be ashamed of.
Come back to class
and this will blow over.

Oh, and by the way,
you left your bag in the hall.
I put it in your locker.
It was decorated
with pads.
I peeled them off.
You're welcome."

"Are you done?"

"No," she says.
"One more thing.
 Stop being such a baby."

BABY

At home that night
I open all my socials
and I mute Harriet
on every one of them
then set my phone
to silent.
I don't want to hear
from anyone again
until morning.

I curl into Mum
while she reads
a lab report
on the sofa,
and I weep,
cradled in the crook
of her body,
like the baby
Harriet says I am.

Mum holds me close,
waits as I sob
then dry my eyes
enough to speak.

Then finally
I tell her everything
Harriet did, like about her

sexting Mr B,
texting me during class,
taking a photo of me in the shower
and pretending to send it to Mr B.

I tell her everything
Harriet did, but I leave
out all the
stuff about me
and Benjamin.
(Obviously.)

There's plenty
for Mum to be
really shocked,
which makes me feel better.

"That all sounds quite serious,"
Mum says. "I expect that's
why Lola grounded her."

"How do you know that?"

"I heard Lola shouting at her.
I hope they're both OK.
Has something happened
to make Harriet act this way?"

"No," I say, annoyed with
her for being so reasonable.
So understanding.
So kind to Harriet.
The bitch.

"Everything is caused
by *something*," says Mum.

I wish she wasn't always
so rational.
"Can I stay at home
tomorrow?" I ask.

"No," Mum says. "You're not ill.
Besides, you're seeing Mr B.
He'll have read your application."

I was so excited
about that, before.
But not any more.
Now I'm just going
through the motions.

"Can I take lunch tomorrow?"

"Of course," she says.

"I still don't want to go in."

"Just talk to her about it,"
she says, like I knew
she would eventually.
"Or do you want me to
knock and talk to Lola?"

"No!" I shout, because
Harriet might have told
her mum *everything*.

211

"Don't talk to her at all.
Even if you see her.
Otherwise I'll never tell you
anything ever again."

"OK," she says,
drawing a cross on her heart.
"Do you want me to
read your application?"

"No," I say. "It's OK.
It's basically ready.
I just need Mr B's
reference tomorrow."

"That's my girl."

I smile,
but I'm not really sure
what kind of girl
she thinks I am.
Nor what kind of girl
I actually am.

I pick up my phone
instinctively thinking
about discussing it
with Harriet
before remembering
we're not talking.

Then our fight
repeats on me,

weighs down on me,
horribly.

And instead I go to bed
feeling heavy
and wondering whether
Harriet and I
can ever
get back
to being
best friends again.

                                    After all,
                                      to her,
                                 I'm nothing.

SEEING RED

My phone is vibrating:
my morning alarm?

Muscle memory
makes me reach
out my fingers.
I try to snooze it,
but it won't stop.

There's a *ting*
and a *chirp*
and a *ding*.

Notifications
come firing in.
I open my eyes
and blink at the screen.

And all I see is
red.

Almost every app
has a little red dot
like a gunshot wound.

WTF?

MEME

Someone
has made
a meme
of me.

I GOT FINGERED ON MY PERIOD

The picture of me   A
I sent to Benjamin.   picture
(The one that Harriet   of two
took under the   bloodied
ice rink car park trees.) fingers.

AND I BLOODY LOVED IT

CHOICES

7.31 a.m.
"Frankie! I'm making porridge."

> My favourite.
> Mum's only in the kitchen,
> but she's light years away.
> I hug my knees
> and try
> and try
> and try
> not to cry.

7.35 a.m.
"Have a good day, Frank!"
Dad shouts.

> He slams the door,
> leaving,
> not knowing
> I'm breaking.
> I can't go to school today.

7.39 a.m.
"Frankie! It's ready!
Shall I bring some to you?"

> "No!" I shout.
> Like a flash, I'm moving.
> "I'm coming down."

I get dressed,
use cover-up
around my splotchy,
blotchy,
puffy
eyes.

I grab some tampons
then go downstairs.
There's no point crying.
No point saying I'm too ill to go in.
I pick up my bag.

"I have to go in early
to see Mr B," I lie.
It's surprisingly easy.

"You still need to eat,"
she says, putting down
her spoon.

"I'll have this on the way,"
I say, grabbing a banana,
trying not to face her.

"What about your teeth?"

"Brushed them already."

"Don't forget your lunch!"
She points to a box
on the kitchen worktop.

She's made me
a packed lunch,
just like she used to
for primary school.
"Thanks, Mum," I say.

She's cut my sandwiches
four ways.
It makes
my heart ache.

"I'm proud of you,"
she calls after me.

If only she knew.

HOW BAD CAN IT BE?

Outside, I let myself feel it.
My feet pound the pavement,
rage and injustice
boiling up from a place
I didn't even know existed.

I only sent that picture
to Benjamin.
So I know
      this was him.
No one has had my phone.

I swipe past the hundreds
of notifications to call
            Benjamin.

It   r i n g s
and   r i n g s
and   he   doesn't   a n s w e r .

He said he didn't mind.
He said it's *biology*.
He said, "It's only blood."

Then he told someone?
Sent them that picture of me?
How dare he ignore me?

I pass the railings of the park
where only the other morning,
Benjamin stopped
          and kissed me.

I look down at my phone
and see the pictures again,
placed beside one another,
making me seem
so disgusting,
and another wave of self-loathing
washes over me.

I crouch in an alleyway
and read everything,
my blood boiling,
until I've seen it all
and it's part of me.

I'm revolting.

I might as well just go to school
and get the reference I need.
How bad can it be?

HOW BAD IT CAN BE

I go through the gate.
        The static crackle of
        goSSip
        flows ahead of me.

The crowd parts slightly,
laughter and hollers
following me.

Marie shoulders her way
out from a group
to walk with me.

"You're in!" she exclaims.

                                    "Yeah," I say.

"I can't believe it."
She links my arm.
"I didn't think you'd come."

                        "What did you think I'd do?"
                        I ask, genuinely interested,
                            because I have no idea
                            how to handle this.

"Stay at home.
That's what I'd do.
You're so brave."

"Where's Harriet?" I ask.

"She's over there."
Marie nods behind her.
"Don't talk to her,
it'll only make it worse."

I wonder for a second
what she means
but then I see Harriet

talking to Leylah
and she sees me
and

even though she must know
what's happened

she turns her back on me
and walks off without Leylah.

My heart sinks.
Is Harriet still
not speaking to me?

"Ignore her," says Marie.

But I'm barely listening,
because all I'm thinking
is how I need
Harriet now,
but I don't think
I'd be able to get
the words out.

Marie leads me
through the crowd,
staring everyone down.

                                    "Why are you
                          being nice to me?" I ask.

"Because you don't
deserve this," she says.

                                 "Thanks, Marie.
                          Have you seen Benjamin?"

She shakes her head.
"What a blabbermouth.
If he is here,
he's going to get
a load of shit from us.
He did leak it, didn't he?"

                                   "Well, *I* didn't tell
                            anybody," I say, numbly.

"That's what we thought,"
she says, nodding.
"And Harry,
she's getting shit from me
today too."

                                     "Thanks," I say.
                          It's nice at least she can see
                                   that right now,

                                        what I need
                                   is my best friend.

Then the bell goes
for registration and I stand there,
searching for Benjamin,

but I don't see him.

UNDER SIEGE

After a hellish registration,
I slip into an empty classroom
and lean against a year seven display
of medieval battle strategy,
checking my phone
for the hundredth time.

It's only been a few
seconds since I last looked,
but there is more.

There
    is
       so
          much
             more.

There's a <u>link</u> in
my DMs
from someone I don't know.
I click it, my skin prickling.
A page loads on
a site I don't know
with a sidebar of threads
slut-shaming celebs.

My page of shame's name:
Freaky Frankie Fanny Fun

Randy^^Tts
    <u>this dirty little schoolgirl</u> has no shame
    lets teach her a lesson

B0rg3n
    wanna finger fck this <u>slut</u> & sm. SGILF

Mazzter
    creamin myself over this lil bitch

I cannot breathe.
I cannot see.
       I have no idea
              what
                    to
                           do.

But then
I hear
the sound
of footsteps,
growing louder,
coming closer
to me.

Lessons will be starting soon
and here I am in the history room,
under siege.

There's a door behind me.
A cupboard.
I duck in
and close it

just as
a class
files in
so
I'm in
the dark
with
old textbooks
squatting
quietly
balancing
silently
carefully
desperately
hoping not
to be
discovered
here in this
dark
little cupboard
hiding
from my own
shame
for
an hour
or more.

Then,
finally,
the chairs scrape,
the door bangs,
the noise of the room
diminishes

to silence
and I open
the cupboard a crack
to check the coast is clear.

It's physics right
after morning break.

I listen
as the volume
rises then falls
in the corridors
and at
the very
last moment,
I make a dash for it.

I need my reference,
then I'm going home.

NUCLEAR DECAY

In physics, there's no space
next to Marie, so I sit at the front.
Maybe Mr B can protect me.

There are whispers and giggles of
"slut" and "period" until finally
Mr B comes in and tells Jackson to
sit down and stop clowning around.

We're doing nuclear decay today,
but I'm not staying.

> I've got my own toxic waste.
> This meme has poisoned me
> invisibly.
> It will never go away,
> just slowly fade,
> halving exponentially.

I simply need the right moment
to ask for the reference,
before saying I have to leave.

"Jackson, do the handouts,
please," orders Mr B.

Jackson gets up, and smirks at me
as he passes and trips over.

"Watch it, dirty," he whispers,
  slapping my back.

                          I hear a rustle
                    as something sticky
                      is attached to me.
                  I reach my hand around,
                        and peel it off.
                    Then bring it back,
                          to look at it
                      under the desk.

                            A pad.

                          It's so stupid
                        I should laugh,
                    but I can feel tears
                  start to well in my eyes.

                      I stand up quickly,
                hitting my thighs on the desk.
                "Sir, I feel faint. Can I leave?"

"Oh," says Mr B. "Do you want
  someone to take you to
  the office?" he asks.

                        "I'll be fine," I say,
                          swinging my bag
                            onto my back,
                        already at the door,
                                but

he calls,
"Don't forget this!"

                                        so I have to come
                                        back into the room
                                        with everyone sniggering

to take the reference
from his hand.

"I read your application.
It's amazing. Feel better."

                                        Somewhere inside
                                        I register what he's saying

but then Jackson shouts,
"Heavy blood loss
can make you feel faint."

                                        And I feel
                                        disgusting again.

And it is the smallest comfort
that I hear Mr B saying,
"Jackson, it is not
acceptable to be heckling
fellow students.
Take a seat
and see me
after class."

POINTLESS ADVICE

I google *What to do if you go viral*
but the answers make out like
it would be a *good thing*.

In PSHE Mrs Lovelie said,
    "If you're getting bullied online,
    remember CRI.
    Confront. Record. Inform."

Who am I meant to *Confront*?
I don't know the people
piling in on me.

Why would I *Record* it?
It's already everywhere.

And *Inform* who?
Mrs Lovelie?

I imagine sitting down
in her little room,
and explaining how

after school
(with my nightclub thighs)
Benjamin Jones
fingered me
on my period
then told everyone.
And someone made a meme,

which has gone viral,
so I'm getting filthy
messages from strangers.

She probably doesn't even
know what a meme is.

There is still Benjamin.
I could confront him.
He's the only one I sent
the picture to, after all.
He either made the meme,
or gave someone else
that picture of me.

DOORSTEP

Benjamin's house
has a red front door.
I approach it slowly,
watching for signs
of life through the windows,
but everything's still.

I walk up the path
and knock
and wait
on the concrete step,
hoping his mum or dad
won't answer, because
all my anger is lined right up,
ready to fire.

                              I watch a silhouette
                              approach through
                              the foggy glass,
                        and feel his imminent
                        proximity in my guts.
                        I take a step back,
                  as though I've been punched.

Benjamin opens
the door a crack,
and looks at me
like he can't believe
I'm here.

"Frankie," he says,
looking behind me,
checking the empty street.
"What are you doing?"

"Well, I couldn't talk to
you in school, could I?
You coward."

"Ah, man," he groans,
his hands on his face.
"You went? I'm sorry.
I just couldn't handle it…"

"You couldn't handle *it*,
or *me*?"

"No," he says. "It's not like that.
I'm not ignoring you.
I wanted to talk."

"Well, here I am.
What did you want to say?
Sorry for bragging to all your mates?
Or for sending my picture
around to all the boys?
Or was it *actually* you?"

"Please," he says,
checking the street again.
"Come inside
and we can talk."

I want to talk to him,
but not in his house.
Not on his terms.

"I've been calling you
all morning."

"I don't have my phone,"
he says. "My parents took it.
And they won't be giving it back
any time soon.
They're ridiculously strict
about school."

"What? Why?
Do they know?"

"No," he says, quickly.
"I tried to bunk off this morning.
But they caught me.
Made me go to school."

"Then where were you?"

"I hid by the library
then came straight home
when they went out.
I've seen how this shit goes down.
There was no way I was going
to school after that meme."

"*I* did."

"How was it?"

"It was horrible.
No thanks to you.
I can't believe you
blabbed our secret.
It was private."

"I didn't tell Jackson!"

"You must have told someone!"

"I promise,
I didn't tell
a soul in school."

"Stop lying!
You were the only one
who knew about what we did."

He says his parents
have his phone,
but maybe he just
doesn't want me
to look on it.

Maybe it's in his pocket
with evidence on it.

He probably sent it
to the boys' group message.
Bragged about fingering me.

"Frankie," he says,
 reaching out,
  trying to touch me.
"Please come in.
 Let's not talk
  about this out here.
 You have to believe me.
 I haven't told anyone
  in school
  anything."

                              "Well Jackson
                          seems to know everything!"

"I didn't tell him!"

                              I don't believe him.
                          "And how did they know
                           about my period starting?
                           I didn't tell anyone that either."

"What, not even Harriet?"

                              "No. We're not talking."

"But…
        Frankie…
                 Harriet made the meme."

DRIFTING

Harriet made the meme.

I'm punched in the stomach,
knocked from my orbit.
Set adrift
spiralling
aimlessly,
helplessly.
I cannot speak.
I cannot breathe.
I cannot see.

"Didn't you know?"
Benjamin says,
taking a step closer to me.
Reaching out to touch me.

I step back,
stagger,
stumble,
mumble,
"No, I didn't know."

"She was the first
to post it."
Benjamin looks worried.
"Frankie," he says.
"Do you want to come in?
You don't look well."

I swallow and blink
and think of how
to get away.
I need to see this
for myself.
"I'm fine," I say, turning around.
"I'm going home.
I'll see you soon."

"I'm sorry," he says.
"I thought you knew.
I promise I didn't brag
about this, Frankie."

My feet are walking
my brain is whirring
and my hands are fumbling
in my school bag
for my phone.

Benjamin calls after me,
"I can help.
I'm going to help.
I'll get it sorted."

But I'm not listening.
His voice fades
as I drift away,
sniffing and scrolling,
head down,
tears falling,
to see for myself.

CRUMBLING

I round the corner
then stop and wipe
my tear-splattered screen
on the soft of my shirt,
and click on Harriet's page.

And there it is.
Posted last night,
when Harriet
was at home
on her own.
I muted her,
so I didn't see
that it was Harriet
who did this to me.

This is why Marie
said she'd give Harriet
shit for me.

I let out a sob
as my knees buckle
and I slide to the concrete
and my insides crumble.

HARRIET DID IT?

Harriet did it?

Harriet who
on the first day of nursery
wet herself because I did
out of pure solidarity?

Harriet who
saved up her pocket money
to buy me my favourite
My Little Pony?

Harriet who
hid behind the trees
when I had my first kiss
(with Elliot Miller)
in case I needed her
to rescue me?

Harriet who has lived next door
my whole life,
who knows everything about me,
and knows how much this would hurt me?

> Did she just do it
> to deflect attention
> from her selfie
> to Mr B?

Harriet was
that angry
with me?

I can't *quite* believe it.

HARRIET DID IT

I get up and walk home,
my heart hurting,
my temples pounding.
Harriet did say,
"You're nothing to me,"
but I still can't believe
that all those years
all those secrets
and moments shared
really don't mean anything to her.

I reach our street and
glance at Harriet's house
right next door
and think about all the times
we've fought before.

Once at the school fair
we agreed to get our
faces painted like bumblebees.
I went first then she backed out
and claimed she never
said she'd do it.
We had a massive fight.

And once, she cut the tail
off one of her own My Little Ponies
then told her mum it was me.

All I did was tell her not to
cut it in the first place.

She did break
Marie's privacy
telling everyone
about her period
being heavy.

And she took
that shower picture
of me.

I guess she *is* this mean.

LOW

I open my phone
and send her a message.

Me
This is a new low,
even for you.

And I watch it
          and watch it,
waiting to see
when it's been delivered,
when it's marked read.

But it doesn't change.
She's still in class
but maybe she's also muted me.
Or blocked me completely.
Deleted me?
I don't know if I'd even
be able to see.

Maybe
to her
I really am nothing.

GONE

In my room
I scroll and scroll,
checking to see
the time stamps on all the posts.

But I can't find any
before the one I saw
on her page.
I go back to look at it,
but then
      I can't find it.
            It's gone.
                I check again.
      I search and search.
~~She's deleted it.~~

I don't know what to think.
Maybe she regretted it?
But that doesn't make
me feel any better.
It's too little too late.
It's **everywhere** already.

I hide my phone
under my pillow
where it can't hurt me,
but I can still feel
the lump of it
pressing into me,

begging me to
look at it.

I move away,
lie on the floor
and try not to think
about how much
Harriet
has
hurt
me
but it's the only thing
I can think about.

She might have deleted it,
but it's not gone.
I still can't believe
she actually did it.

I
simply
can't
believe
it.

A CHANGE OF SCENE

Mum and Dad arrive home together,
and ask me why I haven't been
answering my phone.
(Which is ironic
as they're always telling me
to get off it.)

I briefly worry
that they've seen
the meme,
but if they had,
I'd know by now.

They ask
if I fancy pizza out,
a Friday night treat.

I wonder if we'll see
anyone from school.
But I say yes anyway,
because I really need
a change of scene.

PIZZA

The smell of baked dough
envelops me, as the waitress leads us
to a table
near the open kitchen,
pizza oven full of orange flames.

The waitress gives us menus
and as she takes our drinks order
she looks at me,
her head cocked to the side,
like she's trying
to place me.

                    And I find I'm sweating.
                              OMG.
              Let her not be trying to place me.
              Let her not recognize me.

Mum and Dad talk about
the climate,
plastic,
Brexit,
and I try to join in
but I can feel my phone
in my pocket
buzz buzz buzzing.

The rule is
no phones when we're eating,

                                    but I take it out
                        and try to read it on my lap
but Dad is on me.
"So what's new with you?"

                                    "Nothing," I lie,
                                but my insides writhe.
                                Maybe I'm just hungry.

"And how's Hairy?"

                                    Her name stings.
                                "We don't call her that
                                            any more."

"What's wrong with *Hairy*?
It's the perfect nickname for her.
That girl has so much hair!"

He laughs,
but Mum has the decency
at least
to roll her eyes in empathy.

"Did anything happen with
that boy she was texting?"
he asks, eyebrows waggling.

                                    "Dunno," I shrug.

"Have you two
still not made up?"
Mum asks.

                                        "No," I say.

"You really should talk,"
Mum says.

Then the waitress is back saying,
"Are you ready to order?"
and looking at me,
her head cocked again,
like she's about to ask
whether she knows me.

                                I order quickly
                        and hand her my menu:
                                her signal to leave.
                        Then look at my phone
                                on my lap again
                                until she goes.

"Who're you texting?"
Dad asks, leaning over.

                                "No one," I say,
                                putting it away.

"Have you got
a boyfriend?"
he says.

Mum elbows him.
"She'll tell us
if she wants to."

"If she'd be friends with
me on Facebook,
I wouldn't have to ask."

                              "No one puts anything
                              on Facebook any more."

"Doesn't stop you looking at it
five hundred times a day," he says.
"Anyway, I post things on there."

                              "Exactly," I say.

"Hairy's friends
with her mum."

                              "Just because they're *friends*,
                              doesn't mean she lets
                              her see anything.
                              And I told you,
                              no one calls her
                              Hairy any more.
                              It's Harry or Harriet."

"Oh, come on," protests Dad.
"You're always on your phone.
And you're not talking to Hair—
Harriet. I just thought you might
have a boyf."

                              "Ugh!" I shudder. "Daaaad.
                              You don't say *boyf*."

"Why not? I'm only asking.
It would be sweet
if you did."

                                        Sweet?
                                    The truth
                                        would
                                    crush him.

                        "I haven't got a boyfriend."

"Promise me you'd tell me
if you did?"

                                    "Sure, Dad," I say.

He smiles
and looks so happy

                                    I actually feel OK
                                for the first time today.

The waitress lowers
a veggie feast in front of me,
then she looks at me
and her face changes.

            She's placed me.

"Hey! Aren't you—"

                                    "Thank you," I say,
                            taking the pizza quickly,
                            panic washing over me.

"that girl—"

254

                                    I cough,
                              nodding frantically
                                 at my parents.

"from…"
She glances
at my mum and dad
              and trails off,
                        finally understanding.

"Sorry,
thought you
were someone else!"
she says, doing a good
impression of breezy.
"Enjoy your food."

THAT GIRL

My hands are slippery
on my cutlery.
I cut up my pizza,
and force it down quickly.
My stomach feels crampy.
I glance around nervously.
I just want to be
back at home,
in my room,
hiding from reality.

Mum and Dad
eat painfully slowly,
then order dessert,
and *then* coffee,
and the evening
stretches ahead of me
like an infinity.

I go to the loo
to check my phone
          and there's the waitress,
          drying her hands.

"I'm so sorry," she says,
 touching my arm.
"You're that girl from
 the period meme,
 aren't you?"

I nod.

"I go to King Edward's,
in town.
We've all seen.
Someone said
you're from around here.
You poor thing."

The kitchen bell pings.
"Better go," she says,
her hand on the door.

"By the way,
I think it's really unfair
            what's happening to you."
She smiles kindly.

"You should say something.
Don't let the trolls win."

She pulls the door open.
The smell of pizza
mingles with the chemical
peach of toilet cleaner.

Back at the table,
and later,
in my room,
her words linger.

Not "What's happened to you"
            but "What's *happening* to you."

THE WEIGHT OF WORDS

I wake in the middle of the night
with a horrible dream
clinging damply to my skin.

> *I was watching my friends,*
>> *Harriet,*
>> *Marie,*
>> *Leylah,*
>> *Bethany,*
> *watching a screen.*
> *On it was me.*

> *They were all cheering*
> *as horrible things*
> *were happening to me.*

> *And I was just watching,*
> *doing nothing.*

I go to the window,
fuelled by the freedom
of being awake
in the dead of night.

I open it, lean out
and let the breeze
blow away
the clammy weight
of my bad dream.

At the end of the garden,
up in the leaves
of the sycamore tree,
a light is glowing.

What is Harriet
doing up there
at this time of night?
Maybe she can't sleep
because she's actually
feeling guilty?
            She should be.

I can't believe
all the things she's done
recently.

Like sending that selfie
to Mr B.

And taking that picture
of me in the shower
after PE.

And laughing about
Marie's heavy periods
in front of everybody.

And posting that
horrible meme.
She doesn't think about
the consequences.
She doesn't take responsibility.

Even if she regretted it
and deleted it.
She still did it.

I check my phone
and I can't believe it,
but there's a message
from Harriet.

Harriet
It wasn't me.

I glance up at the tree
and feel in my fists
all of the things Harriet
has done to me recently.

This **pathetic text** is all
she can say to me?

It's so typical of her.
Avoiding taking
any responsibility.

Fury flies from my thumbs
in a frenzy.

Me
Is that really the best
you can do?

Me
You're pathetic.
I know it was you.

Me
I saw it on your page.
Even if you deleted it.

Me
You're such
a fucking liar.

Me
You're nothing to me.

God, it feels good
to get it off my chest.
To say what I think.
To hurt her
like she's hurt me.

I watch as it says

Harriet is typing...

But then she stops.

And I'm stuck, waiting,
staring out of the window
at the green glow
of the lit-up tree house,
amazed my anger
doesn't make
the glass explode.

SAY SOMETHING

I wait for ages,
but Harriet doesn't reply.
I go to my bed
and lie down but I
can't sleep.

I wander mindlessly
onto the page
Freaky Frankie
and read more comments
from people about me.

Some are
supporting me,
but they're all
getting trolled
for being nice to me.
Like that waitress said,
I could say something.

I'm so angry
I start typing.

Oh just fuck off and leave me alone.
You are all saying I'm disgusting. I'm a
slut. I'm a slag. I got my period. Girls get
periods. It's only blood.
Deal with it. #ItsOnlyBlood

I hit *send* and switch off
my phone
and
lie back,
trying to slow my
breathing.

I try to not think
about the meme.

Instead I try
picturing myself
at the planetarium,
handing in
my application
to Vidhi.

I try
to imagine
her face
when she reads
my essay
about black hole
photography.

Or what she'd say
if I got the place.
How it would be
working there
all summer
alongside her.

But the idea
of Vidhi,
the planetarium,
in fact anything
that isn't the meme,

is

beyond me.

TURN ME ON

I wake up early.
I reach for my phone,
feeling hopeful.
Maybe my comment
has changed the way
everyone is
talking about me.

I want to wait,
to savour the possibility,
but it's calling me:

Turn
Me
On.

It's beckoning my fingers
to pick it up
and so I do.

I stroke the screen.
I tap red dots.
It sucks me in.
And all I see are images of me
me
me me me me me me me me me me me me me me me me
me me me me me me me me me me me me me me me me me

me me me me me me me me me me me me me me me
me me me me me me me me me me me me me me me
me me me me me me me me me me me me me me me
me me me me me me me me me me me me me me me
me me me me me me me me me me me me me me me
me me me me me me me me me me me me me me me
me me me me me me me me me me me me me me me
me me me me me me me me me me me me me me me
me me me me me me me me me me me me me me me
me me me me me me me me me me me me me me me
me me me me me me me me me me me me me me me
me me me me me me me me me me me me me me me
me me me me me me me me me me me me me me me
me me me me me me me me me me me me me me me
me me me me me me me me me me me me me me me
me me me me me me me me me me me me me me me
me me me me me me me me me me me me me me me
me me me me me me me me me me me me me me me
me me me me me me me me me me me me me me me
me me me me me me me me me me me me me me me
me me me me me me me me me me me me me me me
me me me me me me me me me me me me me me me
me me me me me me me me me me me me me me me
me me me me me me me me me me me me me me me
me me me me me me me me me me me me me me me
me me me me me me me me me me me me me me me
me me me me me me me me me me me me me me me
me me me me me me me me me me me me me me me
me me me me me me me me me me me me me me me
me me me me me me me me me me me me me me me
me me me me me me me me me me me me me me me
me me me me me me me me me me me me me me me
me me me me me me me me me me me me me me me
me me me me me me me me me me me me me me me

me me me me me me me me me me me me me me me me
me me me me me me me me me me me me me me me me
me me me me me me me me me me me me me me me me
me me me me me me me me me me me me me me me me
me me me me me me me me me me me me me me me me
me me me me me me me me me me me me me me me me
me me me me me me me me me me me me me me me me
me me me me me me me me me me me me me me me me
me me me me me me me me me me me me me me me me
me me me me me me me me me me me me me me me me
me me me me me me me me me me me me me me me me
me me me me me me me me me me me me me me me me
me me me me me me me me me me me me me me me me
me me me me me me me me me me me me me me me me
me me me me me me me me me me me me me me me me
me me me me me me me me me me me me me me me me
me me me me me me me me me me me me me me me me
me me me me me me me me me me me me me me me me
me me me me me me me me me me me me me me me me
me me me me me me me me me me me me me me me me
me me me me me me me me me me me me me me me me
me me me me me me me me me me me me me me me me
me me me me me me me me me me me me me me me me
me me me me me me me me me me me me me me me me
me me me me me me me me me me me me me me me me
me me me me me me me me me me me me me me me me
me me me me me me me me me me me me me me me me
me me me me me me me me me me me me me me me me
me me me me me me me me me me me me me me me me
me me me me me me me me me me me me me me me me
me me me me me me me me me me me me me me me me
me me me me me me me me me me me me me me me me
me me me me me me me me me me me me me me me me

me me me me me me me me me me me me me me me me
me me me me me me me me me me me me me me me me
me me me me me me me me me me me me me me me me
me me me me me me me me me me me me me me me me
me me me me me me me me me me me me me me me me

over and over

only now
my own
words,
my attempt at a defence,
plaster the meme.

"I'm disgusting."
"I'm a slut."
"I'm a slag."

Why did I
write it
like that?

There's a page called
TOP 13 PERIOD GIRL MEMES
and on every one,
my picture has been changed
in some horrible new way.

And in all of them
are the two pictures

next to each other
as though they
belong together.

The picture Harriet took of me
and
those bloodied fingers.

I don't even know
whose hand that is.
A stranger's fingers
supposedly fingered me.
It's so disgusting.
So creepy.

My shaming is still accelerating
like the universe,
getting **bigger**
faster
drawing its energy
from dirty
little
me.

FRIENDS

I check my messages,
hoping there'll be
something from Benjamin.
There's nothing.

He said his parents have his phone
but he could find another way to
message me.
Say he's sorry.
It's still his fault
that people know
what happened between
us that afternoon.

He can't even admit it.
He's no better than Harriet.

I think of mine and Harriet's fight
in the toilets at school.
How she suggested
simply denying
that it was her who sent
the email to Mr B.

This is classic Harriet.
It wasn't me.

Deny it.
Avoid it.
Don't take responsibility.

I do have texts
from all the girls,
who message me separately,
avoiding BEANS ON TOAST
where it would obviously
be awkward.

They're asking if I'm OK.
Telling me that Harriet denies
it was her who posted it.
That they don't believe her.
But it's all so gossipy.
I haven't got the energy
to reply, to say how hurt
I'm feeling.
I feel so lonely.

I want to talk to someone.
But there's no one.
I can't tell my mum
or my dad.
I can't talk to my friends.
Or Benjamin.
I've lost Harriet.

I shove my phone
in my bag
and go downstairs
for breakfast.

PLANETARIUM

Dad gives me a lift.
I sit in the passenger seat,
smoothing the brown
A4 envelope
on my lap.

The summer placement feels
like the only thing
I have going for me
in the whole world.

We pull up outside.
There's a queue already,
children and families
in broad daylight,
waiting to see
the night sky on the
domed ceiling inside.

"Good luck, Frank," says Dad,
as I close the car door
and spot a group of girls
I think go to King Edward's.
They're staring at me.
Nudging. Whispering.

I look down,
but as I pass them
one of them points at me.

I hear a muttered
"Period meme."
I hurry past
the rest of the queue
not looking.

I go inside the cool atrium,
passing the posters
reminding people
to look outside
at the blood moon
next week.

My heart thuds painfully
inside me.

I look for Vidhi
to hand over
the envelope.
I spot her by the desk
near the solar system.
She looks up from her phone.

"Oh," she says,
her mouth falling open.

                              "Hey," I say,
              holding out my application.

But she doesn't take it.
She looks around
and says,

"Didn't you see
Elaine on your way in?"

"No," I say, glancing behind me.
Elaine hasn't spoken to me
since she interviewed me.
I don't think she even
knows who I am.

"Right," Vidhi says,
fiddling with her rings,
then gets her walkie-talkie
and says, "Elaine, could you come
to the ground floor?"

She turns to me.
"Frankie," she says. "I'm sorry.
She should have phoned you."

"What is it?"
I try to read her face.

"Best wait for Elaine."

We stand in awkward silence.
I slide the envelope
behind my back.
I wonder if I'm
about to get fired.

"Have I done
something wrong?"
I say, eventually.

Vidhi bites her bottom lip.
"Elaine doesn't think
you should be in today …
what with *everything* *online*."

                                        "Oh," I say.
                                 I don't know why,
                                    but I thought
                                     that stuff
                                 wouldn't penetrate
                                      this place.
                               Everything about it
                            seems so disconnected
                               from the Internet.

Vidhi leans in and says,
"Sorry, I don't know
how she knows.
Her son's at St Matthew's High.
I think maybe he showed
it to her."

                              My throat starts to close.
                                     "You've seen?"

"Yes," she says.
"I'm sorry. I…
It's horrible."

                                I'm going to cry.
                               The closest exit
                             is just behind Vidhi.
                              I move towards it

just as Elaine comes
              down the stairs.

"Frankie!" she calls,
stopping me
at the door.
"Good, Vidhi told you?
No hard feelings?
We'll get your shift covered
for a couple of weeks."

                              I feel so stupid,
                               my application
                               behind my back.
                    I have to get out of here.
                           My chest trembles.

                                 "Yeah," I say.
                            My voice is weak.
                              "No, it's fine."

"We have quite a conservative
funding body …
and there are children,"
Elaine says, cocking her head
and wincing.
"Parents might complain
if they recognize *your face*.
It's just temporary."

Vidhi moves closer,
reaching out to touch
my arm, but

                            tears are coming,
                          so I push the door
                         and say in a hurry,

"Honestly, it's fine,
I understand.
Thanks anyway.
See you soon."

Vidhi says, "Take care of yourself,
Frank—"
but the fire escape
clicks shut,
cutting her off.

A LONELY UNIVERSE

I lean against the door
of the planetarium,
my hands shaking,
staring down at
cigarette stubs
on the ground,
my application
wavering
in front of me.

Tears tumble off my cheeks
splashing onto brown paper,
making my name
an inky stain.
I feel so lonely.

My body presses
against the
planetarium door.
But the weight of it
pushes back at me
as though it's expelling me.

Inside that building,
the stars are all shining
neatly in their places.
An orderly twinkling
of constellations.

Ursa Major.
Ursa Minor.
Cassiopeia.
Pisces.
Pegasus.
Perseus.
Lyra.
Aries.
Hercules.

I'm on the other side.
I feel
so empty,
like even
the universe
has given up on me.

INSTEAD

I hide
in the trees
behind the car wash
clutching the brown envelope.

The smell of industrial soap
and wax wafts over me
every few minutes
as I cry, on and off,
defiance fighting despair
inside me.

I take out my phone,
thinking about asking
Dad to pick me up early.
Maybe I'll say I'm ill...
  But there are
  so
  many
  notifications
and I don't want to
see them but also
I can't help but read them.
I want to know
what's happening.

It starts to rain,
and I shuffle further
under the trees

hoping nobody sees me.
I'm pathetic,
hiding in the bushes,
shivering,
reading horrible comments
about me.

I'm actually
starting to feel ill.

My phone beeps
and I click on my texts
hoping
there'll be, maybe,
a message from Harry

(She said,
"You're nothing to me.")

or Benjamin.

But it's just low battery.

I wish he'd message.
Or somehow contact me.

Maybe everything
would feel better
if only he'd just admit
he told somebody.
Because he must have.
And now he's ghosting me.

Instead I get
sucked into

a long thread
which someone has tagged me in
where people are discussing
online shamings,
and "Internet misogyny",
and how teenage girls
are "objectified sexually",
      when my screen goes

                           black.

      It's dead.

So now I can't even
call Dad, and instead
I crouch under the trees
in the rain for the
remaining hour,
watching a blinking
digital clock
in a nearby car
until it's time
to go around the front
and be picked up.

When I stand,
I realize I'm still holding
the envelope
with my application in.
It's soaking.

I shove it
into a nearby bin
and dry my eyes,

preparing my lie
to explain why
I'm wet and shivering.

VIRAL

"I think I'm coming
down with something,"
I tell Dad
as soon as I get in the car.
"My throat is sore."

"Oh, you poor thing,"
he says, feeling my forehead.
"Sorry I'm a bit late.
I tried to call.
Why didn't you wait inside?"

"Battery," I mutter.
"Didn't want you
to have to get out
and find me."

Dad turns the heaters on,
making the car
claustrophobically warm,
but at least he doesn't
ask me questions,
especially about handing in
my application.

Mum frowns
as I enter the hall
with Dad's arm around me.
"What happened?
Are you OK?"

"No." I sniff, wiggling my feet
out of my wet shoes.
"I don't feel well."

"It was my fault," says Dad.
"I was late."

Mum reaches out to feel
my forehead too.
I don't know
what they glean
from doing this,
but it is quite comforting.
"You do feel warm.
Let's get you into bed."

I let her lead me
upstairs and tuck me in.
She brings me hot soup
and I eat it,
feeling like a fake,
but

I am ill.
I've gone viral.

Shame has entered my bloodstream.
It's passed from digital me
into reality, infecting
and poisoning
living me.

DMs

I don't reply but the girls still
message me directly
saying they're here for me.

But it's not just them
DMing me.
On almost
all my socials
complete strangers
are messaging me.

Bethany
Hey, gorgeous. We were
all just talking about you,
and wanted to say we're
thinking about you.
None of us agree
with what's happening.

you ugly filthy ho
you need to be stopped

Marie
Hey you. Thinking of you.
Hope you're OK?

you slag bet you
were gagging for it

Leylah
We're all going out tonight.
Wanna come? Might make
you feel better to get all
dressed up?

shiiiiit yo a hott piece o ass

They're going out?
With who?
With Harriet?
Do they really believe
that she didn't make the meme?
Who is she saying
it was?

I feel a bit fake,
but I copy and paste
exactly the same message
to all of them.

Me
Thanks, girls.
I'm actually a bit ill,
so staying home.
Have fun tonight. X

Leylah
We'll miss your
pretty face, Frankie.

fml you're disgusting

Marie
Look after yourself.
Love you. X

you whore

Bethany
Just so you know,
Harriet's not coming.
She's not talking
to any of us
any more.

bitch be diiiiirty...

Maybe Harriet's
actually feeling guilty?

I still can't believe
she, of all people,
would do this to me.

And STILL,
even though
she must know
what's happening now,
she's not talking to me.

Her silence says,
"You're nothing to me."

HARRIET

I wake up late,
and lie in bed
listening to Mum and Dad
unpack the dishwasher
in the kitchen,
singing along to a song
on the radio
like they haven't a care
in the world.

I wonder what the girls
did last night.
I wonder what Harriet did.
Who is she even hanging out with?
Maybe she's still grounded.

I check my phone
to see if there's anything
from the girls,
or Benjamin even,
but there's nothing
except the usual abuse.

I read it.
I'm *crushed* by it.
And I can't stop looking at it.

The thing that I don't get
is Harriet.

I trace my fingers across
the pattern of stars
on the case of my phone
and think about her being
angry enough with me
to actually
make
and post
that meme.

I thought I knew her.
I thought I understood her.
I know she can be mean,
but this mean?

I can't believe it.

And

        I can't believe
        how much it
        hurts.

BEANS ON TOAST

No one's written
in the group for days,
but I can see Harriet's online,
and I've got nothing left
to lose, so I write:

Me
Hey girls,
how was last night?

Leylah
Ah, it was so fun!
Hope you're managing to
ignore all the twats online?
They're just joking.

if my girl askd me to do
what you're into
I'd dump her skank ass

Bethany
We met some boys last night
from St Matthew's High
and they were all saying
they knew about you
and thought it was horrible too.
Their school did an assembly
on online bullying, apparently.

Ignore the haters.
They can't harm you.

@mazzymaz @gizmojim We found you @PhysicsFrankie HA. Tried to defend yourself. Pathetic bitch.

Marie
Yeah. It's so horrible.
We're all hoping it
blows over soon.

she can suck me off

Then on the screen it says,

Harriet has left the group.

> Those tiny words
> are cold water
> engulfing my body.
> My heart is sinking.
> She can't say sorry.

Bethany
OMG. She can't leave!

I'd love to do this to her

Leylah

She says she didn't
post the meme.
Maybe we should listen
to her?

that just made me cum

Bethany

If she didn't do it
why did she just leave
our group?

Me

Maybe she's not
talking to me.

Bethany

Don't worry. She's not
talking to anybody.

Leylah

I just think we should
listen to her if she says
it wasn't her.

Bethany

Erm... It was posted
ON HER PAGE???

Quite hard to see how
it could have not been her.
She's always been kinda mean.
I don't believe her.

Marie
I feel bad to say it,
but I don't either.
That thing she said
about my period
was super shit of her.
She's out of control.

Bethany
Exactly. And that
pic she took of Frankie
in the shower.
She definitely made the meme.
It stinks of her.
She just doesn't know
how to say sorry.

what a randy bicth

Marie
How are you, Frankie?
We missed your face
last night.

download here to cum
on her stupid face

Me
I missed you guys too.
Glad you had fun.
Better go. XX

I can't talk about this any more.
I click off the chat.

Then, thinking about Harriet,
I open my stargazing app
and see, above me,
on the other side of the ceiling,
the nearly full moon,
which will soon be
a blood moon.

But without Harriet,
I can't get excited about it.
Even thinking about it
makes me feel shit.

DIGITAL ME

I stay in my room
almost all day.
Mum and Dad
keep popping in
to see if I'm OK
but there's a universe
between us
and I can't seem
to reach across
the abyss of this
online mess
to ask them
to help me.

I WANT TO STOP BEING

Night-time comes.
I've been in bed
all day.
I feel disgusting
but I can't stop reading,
scrolling,
checking
for more horrid things
being said about me.

I keep thinking
I should go to sleep
and I'm really about to
when I read something

that makes me fling
my phone
across the room.
It whacks the wall,
and I hear the impact
crack the screen.

I crawl
and pick it up again.

It doesn't make
any sense.
Why would someone
write these words?

I read it
over and over,
scared,
because I don't
think they're joking.

My eyes
flood
until tears spill
onto the cracked
surface of my screen.

Someone needs to rape you
you feminist bitch

I can't stop shaking.
My insides are shrinking.
I want to stop being.

I stay dead still
hoping
that
Mum
or Dad
will
come
soon
and check on me
because
if they don't

I'm scared I might
turn into

n o t h i n g . . .

BUNKING OFF

Monday morning
I lie in bed,
flat and grey,
an old jumper
with nothing left
to give.

Dad wants to
call the doctor,
but Mum persuades him
to leave me,
see how I feel
once I'm fully awake.

"Could Harriet

(the treacherous bitch)

pop round after school?"
Dad says.
"Or have you two
still not made up?"

(I don't know if we ever will.
Nothing to me.
Nothing.
Nothing.)

"I'm fine," I say,
pulling the duvet
over my head.
"Just let me sleep."

"We'll call you later,"
Mum says.

"Or you call us," Dad adds.
"Or send us a text.
Anything."

I hear the front door close,
but I stay in bed,
wondering whether Harriet
will ever admit what she did.

And I think about Benjamin.
I wonder what he's doing.
I look at the photo he sent me,
back when everything
with him was dreamy.

Him in bed,
thinking about me.
I feel so stupid,
believing he liked me.
He hasn't even messaged me.

At ten o'clock I get up,
unsteady on my feet,
and go to the lounge,
sit down and cradle

my broken phone
to find out
what's happening
to me now.

I turn on the telly for company
and pull a blanket up for safety,
and I start to read.
I thought it would be
fading by now.
But it's getting worse
somehow.

I have a DM from
someone I don't know
called TheDonaldoBro.
I have so many messages
I haven't even tried
to read them all
but I see the start of this one:

I'm going to find out where you live

so I click
to read the rest

**and I'm going to come
and rape you to teach you a lesson,
you filthy little cunt.**

(NO TITLE)

my
blood
runs
cold

my hands
are   wet
i
cannot
        see

my mouth   fills
with
spit
my   throat is dry
i'm gonna   puke
i want to die

        i want to
leave the internet

take   myself   back
but   i know   it's   too late
            for   that

KNOCK KNOCK

I stare at my phone.

I'm going to find out where you live

Sick creeps up my throat
but then—

KNOCK KNOCK.

Someone is at our door.
My arms are shaking.

KNOCK KNOCK.

What should I do?
Call the police?
Hide?
Weep?

I sweat
and creep
to the window
and peep.

A man
is standing
in our front garden—

KNOCK KNOCK.

He turns his head
and looks right at me
through the window.
He can see me.

My heart
explodes.

Then he waves
a brown box at me.
Mouths *"Delivery."*

I go to the door
and shout,
"Leave it outside!"

"Need a signature, love."
The man's voice
is loud.

"Please!" I beg.
I sound pathetic.

"No can do," he says.

Isn't this
what someone would say
if they were trying
to trick me to let them inside?

I take a deep breath,
shout, "Go away!"
Then I sit on the floor
under the window

                              and listen, waiting
                              to hear him leave.

The letter box clatters,
and his voice comes inside.
"Hello?" he calls.
"You still there?
Are you OK?"

                                   I start to cry.
                                   "GO AWAY!"
                                   I scream.
                              "LEAVE ME ALONE
                         OR I'll CALL THE POLICE!"

I hear the letter box close
and his voice mutter,
"All right, all right."

Then I hear
him knocking on
Harriet's door.
I hear Lola answer.

"Sure, I'll sign for it."

I hear him say,
"Cheers, gorgeous,"
and the sound of his
footsteps fade up the path.

Just a delivery guy.

I feel ridiculous.
Lola is metres away,
but I'm sitting here,
sobbing and shaking.
I can't even talk to her,
because this is all
her daughter's fault

and I'm scared
to go outside.

THE WALKING DEAD

I want my life back.
I want to go outside
and be nobody again:
just a girl, going to school.
Just a girl, doing gym.
Just a girl, walking
with her best friend
to buy croissants
to eat in their tree house
before dawn.

Just a girl,
looking up at the night sky
wondering how we got here
and sighing at
the marvel of life.

I miss my life.
I miss my best friend.

I'm alive.
Yet not alive.
I am the walking dead.

PART
THREE

BUSTED

On Tuesday morning,
my parents decide
my virus has sufficiently
subsided
and I'll survive
a day in school.

I try to persuade them
to let me stay home,
but I don't have a fever
and I can't tell the truth

so I leave the house
and hide in the alley
waiting for what
feels like for ever
for Dad and Mum
to go to work.
Then I scurry home.

But when I open
the front door
Mum is right there.

"Frankie. What's going on?"
Her face is calm,

but this is what it does
before the storm.

                              I reach for a lie:
                              "I forgot my kit."

But she holds up her iPad,
and on it I see
there's an email from school.
"Then why is Mr Adamson
asking me and Dad
to come in for a meeting
tomorrow afternoon?"

                              "I don't know," I say,
                              my insides squirming,
                                    attempting to
                                  escape my body.

Mum says,
"You didn't go in today.
And you didn't finish on Friday.
And what about yesterday?
Were you actually poorly?
I want you to stop lying."

                              I want to stop lying,
                              but how can I tell her
                            what's happening to me
                                        because
                                    I was horny
                              and on my period
                              and a dirty sla—

"Frankie!" she says.
"Whatever it is,
 you can tell me."

                              I shake my head.
                              I *can't* tell her this.
                    I cannot bear for her to know
                                    I got f—

"You can tell me anything.
You're my own
flesh and blood."

Then I notice
there are tears in *her* eyes.

            Why is *she* crying?

                    "I can't tell you, Mum…" I say.
                    But even as I hear my words
              f l o a t   h e r   w a y
                            my hand goes
                        to my shattered phone,
                        and I open the page
                        Freaky Frankie Fanny Fun.
                        She's going to find out anyway.
                        I hand my phone to Mum
                            and turn away.

I can't watch her face
as she sees
all the comments
and pictures

and memes
about me.

But I can't *not*
watch her face
and wonder
which post she is on.

The original meme
    about the period
    fingering?

Or maybe some of the
photoshopped images
where disgusting things
have been done
to the fingers
and to my face.

Then Mum breathes out very loud.
"WHAT IS THIS?" she practically yells.

             I've never seen her face like this:
                 her nostrils flared,
                    her skin tight,
                        white
                    like bone.

               But I can't speak.
               I don't have the words
               to explain what *this* is.

Mum stares at me
so long I wonder if she'll ever speak,
and all I can think is:
how is she
going to love me
after this?

Even my blood
feels cold in my veins,
like it doesn't want to be
part of my shame.

I close my eyes
and look at the dark,
and start to drift apart.

But then I feel Mum's arms
close in on me,
wrapping around
my trembling body,
squeezing me.

I press my head
against her chest,
so close and still
I can hear her heartbeat,
and I let go.

She holds me tightly
as though she's
trying to say:
I can hold you together.

But she must know
she can't.

FAMILY MEETING

Eventually
I stop sobbing,
and she lets go of me
and gets out her phone.

"Mum!
What are you doing?"
I ask, following her to the kitchen.

"I'm calling Dad."

"Why?"

"To ask him to come home.
He needs to see this."

"Mum! No.
This is bad enough, without
sitting around talking about it.
Please don't show D—"

But he's already answered
and Mum's saying,
"Hello, it's me. Do you mind
popping home at lunch today?
 …
  Now is even better.
    …

That's great.

...

See you in five."

"Mum! Send me to my room.
Take my phone away.
Ground me.
Just don't tell Dad.
Please."

"That's not fair, Frankie.
How is he supposed to
understand you,
support you,
if you keep things
from him?"

And there was me
thinking the humiliation
had peaked.

Dad comes home
and walks into the kitchen
looking worried.

I can't cope with the cringe,
so I go to the table and sit down
with my head in my hands,
and listen to Mum explaining
what he's about to see.

I can tell when he's scrolling
by the sounds of his breathing.

I wonder what he's reading,
what he's seeing,
then I hear sniffling.

I lift my head.
"Oh, Dad!" I say.
"Please, don't cry."

"Why would anyone do this?"
he says, wiping his eyes.

I'm not sure what he means by *this*.
What I did?
Or what's been done to me?

And then I wonder,
if my parents
have had an email
from Mr Adamson, will
Harriet's mum have had one too?

I wonder if Harriet
will tell her the truth,
or just pretend
she's innocent?

"Why you?" he asks.

"Why anyone, Dad?" I say.
He's meant to be comforting *me*.
"It's just time-wasters online,
not thinking about
the real life behind

what they're doing."
(And my ex-best friend
leaking my secrets to be mean.)

"But why would so many people
make up all this stuff about you?"

(Because I'm disgusting.)
I shrug.
"It's not all made up."

"What do you mean?"

"The meme at the top.
That's sort of true."

"What's a meme?" asks Mum.

"A picture with words on,
like captions," I say,
my skin prickling
as I start sweating.

Dad scrolls on my phone
then turns it to face me.
"You mean this one?"
He's showing me
the one that says:
"I got fingered on my period
and I bloody loved it."

"That's the one,"
I say as a

                                        gravitational wave of
                                   cringe travels through me,
                                              warping me.

Mum peers around to see.
"Oh, the period thing.
Well, that's nothing
to be ashamed of.
It's only blood.
Gosh, the Internet
is sexist."

But Dad's gone pale
and I wait,
watching his face
as he comes over
and hugs me,
but he doesn't
actually look at me.

"We need to get this
taken down,"
he says.

                                   "Dad," I say. "It's all over
                                              the Internet.
                                       You can't delete it."

"Then we'll phone the police,"
he says into his hands,

                                   not looking at me.

He hasn't looked at me
since he saw the meme.

"We need to report it."

I feel so dirty
hearing those words.
This is so unfair.

"Yes," says Mum.
"I do agree.
We will have to call
the police.
Maybe after we've seen
Mr Adamson."

I knew
they'd say this.
I've looked it up.
"There's basically nothing
the police can do."

"We'll still report it."
Dad sighs,
and runs his hands
down his face.

And I say,
"I'm sorry. This
is all my fault."

"No!" Mum says.
"You haven't done
anything wrong,
have you?"

                              "No." I shake my head.
                              And try to believe it.

"This is not your fault,"
she says, coming over
and holding me.

                              I let her squeeze me
                              and don't try to see
                              what Dad's doing.
                              What he's thinking.

"We're not going to sit back
and do nothing. We're going
to put this right."

                              I wish Dad would say
                              something reassuring,
                              so I know he still accepts me,
                              still loves me.

                              Mum lets go of me,
                              and I look at Dad
                              and say, "Are you mad at me?"
                              My voice is shaky.

"Of course not," he says,
shaking his head.

But I don't believe him.

He stands up
and goes to the sink
and with his back
to me says,
"You were going to tell me
if you had a boyfriend."

I pause, then say,
"He's not my boyfriend."

Oh God.
What must he think of me
that I'd do something
so intimate
with just *anybody*?

It all suddenly seems so dirty.
It really wasn't meant to be.

Mum takes my hand.
"Did *he* do this viral thing?"

"It takes more
than one person
to make something
go viral."

"We do know that," says Mum.
"But did one of you tell someone?"

"I didn't tell anyone."

"We could talk to his parents!"
Dad says, turning round.

"What's that
going to achieve?"
I'm fuming with Benjamin
for blabbing to everyone,
but my parents
talking to his parents
about *this*?
#NoWay

"Please," begs Dad,
"just tell us his name."
As if knowing something
will anchor him.

"Benjamin." I sigh.
"His name is Benjamin.
But he didn't make the meme."

"Then who did?"

I hesitate
then say,
"I don't know who,
but the damage is done."

What would they do
if they knew it was
Harriet who'd brought
all this on me?

"You're right," says Mum, nodding.
"The important thing
is you going back
to school."

                                        "Not today!" I say.

Mum looks at Dad,
and they nod at each other,
agreeing at least
this tiniest mercy
to let me carry on hiding
for one more afternoon.

"You can stay home today," she says.
"But tomorrow, you go in.
And we'll talk to the head
in this meeting."

Dad nods,
but goes to leave the kitchen.
"I'm sorry, Frankie.
I need some space to think."

                                        "Dad!" I cry.
                              "What are you doing?"

"Just give him a moment."

                                        "Oh God," I say.
                      "He's going to look up Benjamin."

"No," says Mum firmly.
"He wouldn't do that."

I feel my chest tightening
as Dad's footsteps fade.
He can't even look at me.
"He's ashamed of me."

"He's not," she says.

But only
to make me feel better.
"I really don't want
to go to school tomorrow."

"You can do this.
You're strong.
And we'll be there
in the afternoon
to support you."

Ugh. She's right.
My *parents* are going to come in.
Everyone is going to know they know.
Everything.

"This is going to be
so embarrassing.
Please don't make me go."

"You can do this,"
Mum says, crouching
in front of me and

holding my arms
reassuringly.
"Are you ashamed?"

I think about it.
I mean
I really
think
about it.

Am I ashamed?
I think back to that afternoon.
To me and Benjamin
stargazing,
talking,
and getting my period
on his fingers.

It was embarrassing,
but not shameful.

The shame has come from
what other people have said.
I can't do
anything about them.

I would do it again.

I shake my head.
"No," I say, "I'm not ashamed."
And as I say it
I feel *fast* and
f r e e

like a particle
that's just been
fired around the
Large Hadron Collider.

I feel like me.

I pick up my phone,
instinctively,

but Mum gently
prises it out of my hands.
"I'd better keep this,"
she says, pocketing it.
"Just until we've
worked out how to
get all this taken down."

DOING SOMETHING

Mum tells me she's going
to check on Dad and
I don't mind.
My thoughts are racing.

I make myself a sandwich
and eat it in the kitchen,
chewing it slowly
trying to think clearly.

I can't hear my parents
speaking, or even moving.
The house is so silent,
incongruous with
my noisy, defiant thinking.

I don't want to retreat
back to my room.
I'm raring to go,
to do something.

I clear up my lunch
and then sit in the kitchen
listening to the tap dripping,
trying not to think of
Dad being ashamed of me,
even if Mum says he isn't.

I bounce my knee
until I can't bear it
and I stand up,
go to the door,
pull on my trainers
and shout,
"I'm going out!"

I surprise myself
as I open the front door
and step outside
into the wide world.

I've got time to kill
before school is out
so I walk away from home
and take a long route
around the houses,
thinking about
what I've gone through,
how much I've been alone,
how impotent it's made me.

I know I'm lucky
to have Mum and Dad
but they can't sort this out.
Their only plan
is to try to take stuff down.
They have no clue.

I think about
the waitress in the toilets
that night who told me

I should say something.
I've been scared to speak
to anybody since it blew up online.

I keep checking the time,
then finally
at four
I turn sharply
and walk quickly
down the street.
I can talk to Benjamin.

I can confront him again.

Now I think about it,
time has given me clarity,
and even though I know
he didn't make the meme,
I do know he told somebody.

It's easy, really,
        one turn here,
                down the next street,
        along a few more,
        and before I know it
I'm looking at his
red front door.

I don't let myself think.
I don't let myself stop.
I just walk up to it,
reach out with my fist
and knock.

FIX IT

I stand still and wait,
braced to deliver
my scathing reproach.
I watch his shadow approach
through the cloudy glass
and then

Benjamin's mum
opens the door
and I'm totally thrown.

"Hello," she says, smiling.

"Er … hi," I say, searching
for words to explain
who I am
and what I'm doing
standing here
looking determined.
"I'm … er …
is … er …
Benjamin in?"
I finally get out.

She tilts her head,
gives a flicker of a grin,
before standing aside
and saying,
"Sure, come in."

My eyes fall straight
on Benjamin's trainers
lying on the floor at
the foot of the stairs.
The same ones he
took off in my hall
right before we got
almost completely naked.

"Go on up,"
she says, pointing
to a door at the top
of the stairs.
"He's in his room."

"Thanks," I mutter,
slipping off my shoes,
the carpet squashing softly
beneath my bare feet.

I climb the stairs,
wondering if my parents
would ever be so cool
about letting a boy
come up to my room.

But before I'm at the top,
Benjamin's mum shouts up,
"Someone's here for you!
Keep the door open!"

And I'm in his doorway,
breathing in the clean,

biscuity-sweet
smell of his room.

Benjamin is lying
on his bed.
"OK!" he shouts
down to his mum,
not looking up
from his laptop,
which is on the bed
next to him.

Rugby kit covers the floor
and on the wall above his head
is a huge poster
of what I know to be
a Cassini mission photo
of Saturn's icy rings.

Benjamin taps the keys

and I look at his screen

and I **freeze**.

Half of the meme
fills his screen.
Not the picture of me,
but the one that's always
next to me with the
bloodied fingers.
Stranger's fingers.

Why is he looking
at that bit on its own?
I feel
disgusting.

A whimper escapes me.

Benjamin turns
and practically
falls off his bed
as he sees me
and scrambles up.

"Frankie!" he says.
"What are you do—"

"What are *you* doing?"
I say, pointing at his screen.
I try to sound strong.
I feel so small.
I wish I hadn't come.
I want to fall
into a black hole.

Benjamin looks from
me to his screen.
Panicking.
Guilty.

I'm so confused.
I know, *know*,
he told someone,
but…

"Did you have something
to do with the me—"

"No!" he says, shaking his head.
"I'm trying to help you!"

I search his face,
wondering how he
could possibly be helping me.

"I can't believe you're here,"
he says, taking a step
closer to me. Then stopping.
"Can I show you
something I've just
found out?"

He pulls the laptop
to the edge of the bed,
kneels on the floor
and starts clicking.

I move a little closer,
watching over his shoulder.
Curiosity silencing my anger.

Then he brings up
reams of white text
against a black screen.

"The metadata
shows where

the fingers photo
was taken."

                                    "It's geotagged?"

"Exactly," Benjamin says,
his eyes wide and hopeful.
"This is not a stock photo.
It was taken just before
the meme was posted.
At about one that morning.
          Locally.
But it was nowhere
near Harriet's house."

                              "Then where?" I say,
                                 my heart lifting,
                                      skipping,
                      as I try to stop myself imagining
                                what it would mean
                                      if the meme
                                          wasn't
                                          Harriet.

"There's only one person
I know who lives
in the area where the
photo was taken."
Benjamin pauses.
He looks worried.
"Jackson."

I blink.
And shake my head,
trying to catch up
with what he's said,
and what it means.

Harriet was grounded.
She'd never go
against her mum.

Did Harriet really not make the meme?

"So…" I say, swallowing.
"Are you saying
Jackson made the meme?"

Benjamin nods

and

I realize I'm standing,
guilt and regret
battling in my guts.
"Harriet hasn't been lying."

"She could have
been with him."

"No," I say, shaking my head.
"She was grounded."
I bend over feeling
almost sick with relief.
I breathe out deeply.
Then breathe in,
trying to take it all in.

I was so angry with her
about the shower photo,
I believed she'd do *anything* mean.
Even the meme.
I didn't listen to her.

But at the same time as
realizing Harriet
didn't make the meme,
I'm realizing that
Benjamin still blabbed
to somebody.
He was the only one
who knew.

"You told Jackson,"
I say, standing up straight
to look at Benjamin.

"I didn't!" he protests.

"Stop lying!" I say,
my voice rising,
hoping his mum
doesn't hear me.

"It was on Harriet's page.
How did he get into
her account if she
wasn't there?"

"Maybe he guessed it?"
I say, thinking about how

all her passwords are
variations of 99 Flake,

and how she was salivating
over her milkshake
when we went ice skating,

and how Jackson knew
her phone's passcode
was 9999.

"Don't ask me how, but
her password would have
been really easy
for him to figure out."

"But that doesn't mean he—"

"Just admit you told
Jackson what we did!"
I snap.
I need to go
and see Harriet.

"I didn't," he says.

"Stop lyin—"

"Wait!" he says, pleading,
his hands on his head,
compressing his curls,
as though he's trying
to force something out.

"I told my sister.
I texted her
when I got home
that afternoon.
I was worried I'd hurt you."

"You told your *sister*?!"
I say, incredulous.

Benjamin nods.
"I didn't know what else to do.
She works weird hours
in California so
she didn't reply
until the next morning.
I was in school.
Jackson read
the message I sent my sister
over my shoulder."

I stare at Benjamin.
Searching his face
to see if he's lying.
Can that really be it?
Something so naive?
So innocent?

"I'm sorry.
I should have told you.
I just hoped so much
it wasn't all my fault.
My sister's been helping me
take the worst stuff down."

I ignore the implication
that there has been worse
than what I've seen.
My temper is rising again.
"That's what my parents
said we should do
when they found out."

"Your parents *know*?"

"They know everything.
They're going in to
see the head tomorrow.

Why didn't you just tell me?"
I'm almost shouting.

Benjamin sighs.
"I'm really sorry.
I couldn't bear it.
I was just pretending
it wasn't my fault.
I felt terrible."

"*You* felt terrible?"
I am shouting now.

"Everything OK?"
Benjamin's mum calls
up the stairs.

"Yes!" he calls back. "Fine!"

But I'm not fine.
I'm furious.
"And you ignored me!"

"My parents have
my phone."

"There are other ways
to contact me,"
I say, nodding at his laptop.

"You're right," he says.
"I just wanted to
fix it for you,
then show you."

I shake my head.
"I didn't need you
to fix it for me.
I just wanted you
to be there for me."

Benjamin looks
genuinely surprised.
"Is that all?"

"That's all."

Benjamin swallows.
His Adam's apple bobs
at the neck of his T-shirt.
"I felt so guilty.

I'm sorry.
I was hiding."

"You were lying."

Benjamin nods.
"I wish I'd just told
you the truth.
I was lying to myself too.
I didn't know what to do.
I really like you."

"I like you too.
But I don't trust you."

Benjamin looks down at his feet,
then up at me.
"Maybe over time
I can gain that back?"
Benjamin says.
"I really hope we can
hang out again."

"I hope so too," I say.
Maybe he was
just ashamed like me.
But I need
time to think.

"Send me that thing,"
I say, pointing
to his screen
as I leave.

I have an idea forming but
before I do anything
I have to talk to Harriet.

AN APOLOGY

I run all the way
from Benjamin's house
my legs working
as hard as my brain
straining to sort
the muddling feelings
of guilt
from shame.

I reach Harriet's gate,
legs aching,
heart pounding,
mouth bursting with
an apology I desperately
hope isn't too late.

Harriet opens her front door
and takes a step back
as she sees it's me.

Her face is red.
Her eyes are puffy.

"Frankie," she says.
"What's happening?"

Sweat is dripping
down my spine

and I'm panting from running
as I blurt out,
"I know you didn't
make the meme."

I stop to breathe,
my throat tightening.

"Jackson hacked you.
Benjamin can prove it."

I lean over
and gasp for breath
then stand back up
and search her face.

Hoping she understands
what I'm saying.

Hoping she won't slam
the door in my face.

Her brow furrows.
She blinks slowly.
Sniffs a little.
"No one believed me."

"We were so angry."

She starts nodding,
sobbing and saying
"It wasn't me" over and over

as though she's making up
for all the time she's been
coping with everyone
thinking it was her.

"Harry," I say,
reaching out to her,
"I'm so sorry."

She looks at me
with her bloodshot eyes,
sniffs snottily and says,
"I did some horrible things,
but I would never do
something so cruel."

"I know," I say, swallowing,
my heart hurting
seeing how much
pain Harriet's in.
"I'm sorry I didn't believe you."
Tears slide
over my hot cheeks.
"I wanted to,
but it was so convincing.
And I was furious with you."

Harriet nods,
tears still pouring
down her cheeks.
"You had every right to be."

"Please forgive me?"

"*Me* forgive *you*?"
Harriet says, wiping
her nose on her sleeve.
"Frankie, I was awful to you.
I took that shower photo.
I pushed you over.
I snapped over
that whole email thing.
It was so embarrassing.
I wanted to get you into
as much trouble as me.
I'm the one who
should be saying
sorry to you."

                "What I said to you in the toilets
                         that day was horrible."

"It was quite mean."

                    "I just didn't understand
                         why you'd send
                         a picture like that."

"I think in my
sleep-addled state I
thought it would make
Mr B like me as much
as he likes you.
I'm not as clever as you."

                         "Harry," I say.
                         "You're so clever.

I'm the idiot.
I shouldn't have judged you
about the email.
I should have just
been there for you."

Harriet winces.
"I should have
been there for *you*.
I didn't know
how to come back to you."

"I didn't either.
But I am so, so sorry."

The afternoon breeze
sweeps the clouds aside
and a sunbeam falls on us,
illuminating us, ridiculously,
both crying snottily,
standing on the doorstep,
tears dripping from our faces.

"I'm more sorry
than I can ever say.
To the moon and back
or something really big
and cheesy like that.
You're not nothing to me.
You're **everything**."

"God, I've missed you!"

"I've missed you too."

Then we hug each other,
squeezing tightly,
sort of laughing,
sort of crying,
and for the first time in ages
I feel like smiling.

So I say,
"My parents saw
my porno debut,"
and I watch her

as her eyes go so wide
they look like they're
about to fall out of her face.

AN IDEA

"OMG, tell me
everything
immediately!"

"I showed them *everything.*"

"*Everything* everything?"

"Everything everything.
Pirate porn.
The *Carrie* one.
The vampire
with the strap-on."

"You didn't edit?"
Harriet says, covering her mouth.

"I couldn't edit!
It's on the bloody Internet."

"Shiiit," she mumbles,
her hands hiding her face.
"What did they say?"

"Well, they took my phone,
for a start."

"No!" Harriet gasps.
"It wasn't *your* fault."

"I know!" I say.
"And they have to go
for a meeting tomorrow
with Mr Adamson."

"And my mum too.
I guess someone told Mr Adamson
about it being on my page."

"That's not fair though!
You didn't do it."

"At least now I can prove it."

"About that," I say.
"I have an idea."

"Tell me!" says Harriet.
"I'm all ears."

GRABBING THE BULL

I wake at dawn,
dread coiled
thickly in my guts
like a wet snake.

> I used to be
> > a *good girl*,
> but what does that even mean?

Today
I *might* get expelled
for what we've planned,
but I'm going to
see this through;
we have a plan,
and I want to
reclaim the truth.

It's laugh or be laughed at.
Kill or be killed.

I get up,
my legs heavy,
reluctant to carry me
even to the bathroom.

I sit on the toilet,
my stomach writhing,
trying to keep me
from going outside.

But I'm going to school
today. I just have
to stick to the plan.

I get ready like normal,
and put everything
I need inside my bag
out of my parents' sight.

I don't tell them
what Harriet
and the girls
and I
planned last night.
There's no point
spinning them out,
or risking them
trying to stop me.
They don't have the answers.

"Ready?" asks Mum.

I nod.

"Good for you, Frank,"
Dad says,

and maybe I'm imagining it
but I'm sure he's still
being weird with me.

I just want him to not
be ashamed of me.

"Be brave," says Mum.
"Fighting problems head-on
can make them melt away.
Grab the bull by the horns."

I'll try.
But there's every chance
I'll end up getting
trampled on today.

"I'm so proud of you,"
she adds.

I know she is *now*.
I'm just not sure if our plan
is exactly what she's
got in mind.

RECLAIMING MY REPUTATION

Harriet and I hide
around the corner
from the entrance
to assembly
while our year
files inside.

"Do you feel OK
about seeing Jackson?"

Harriet nods.
"I'm not thinking about him.
I'm thinking about
Benjamin texting his sister
for sex advice!"

Then we hear a comedy cough.
"That's the signal from Marie.
Everyone is in assembly.
Ready?"

She opens her bag,
and hands me my T-shirt.
"I've got mine on.
Put your hoody on
over the top."

I nod and do it,
but my guts coil up.

She squeezes my hand.
"You are brave,"
she says.

> And when I think about
> what I've been through
> I realize I am.

We walk around the corner
of the building.
A group of girls
from the year above
walk past us, pointing
and whispering,
      "...on her period."

Yesterday that might have
broken me,
but today it seems to
bounce off me.
I won't be shamed
for getting my period.
It's only blood.

Outside the auditorium
Marie is holding an empty
marker pen box
and two paper bags
which flutter in the breeze.

"They've all gone!"
she says excitedly.
"Almost everyone took one.

The printed ones
and the blank ones."

Then Marie grabs me,
hugs me.
"Leylah's inside already."

Suddenly Harriet says,
"Look! Mr Adamson
is coming!"
And we turn to see
Bethany walking with him,
distracting him.

We scuttle in
and slip behind
the long black curtain
which hangs across the stage.

Harriet peeks through the gap

                      but in the muffled silence
                              of the dark
                            I feel uncertain.

                          But I remember
                        Newton's third law.

            For every action,
        there is an equal and
         opposite reaction.

        This is ours.

"You can do this,"
Harriet says, grinning.
"I'll be in the sound booth
at the top."

Then she turns
and leaves.

                              I wait,
                          and just
                          breathe,
                    and it feels
                      as though
                          time
                          slows,
                        warped
                    by the mass
                  of what we're
                  about to do.

Then all the auditorium lights
go off, and I count to three,
then throw myself through
the curtain, into the darkness.

I can see a sliver
of green emergency light
reflecting off Mr Adamson's head
at the side.
He's waiting off stage
and next to him is
Bethany, who has
hopefully persuaded him
to give us a few minutes.

Then Harriet
flips the spotlight on,
lighting the banner behind me.

THIS ASSEMBLY IS
A #NoShame ZONE

And in front of it,
    I am bathed in
        bright
                white
                    incandescent
                            light
        choosing to be seen.
            The real me.

    I've spent
            so much time
                alone online
                        hiding from the world
                        in the silence of my room
                I could never have imagined
            how comforting
        the gentle rustle
        of a crowd of people
could be.

I think about my friends
helping me to organize this.
About Marie blagging
a box of plain T-shirts
from her Dad's business

and the five of us giggling
and scribbling with sharpies
up in the tree house
until early this morning.

And I think about Harriet
at the back now,
supporting me.

I take a deep breath.
I hear the hall wait
for me to say
what I need to say.

Finally I speak.
"I got publicly shamed.
What happened to me
was a nightmare.
I hid and I felt ashamed.
But what did I actually do?"

The noise lifts, then falls from chatter
        to mutters
                to silence
                        as they watch me
                                take off my hoody.

                On my T-shirt,
                    printed out
                and ironed on,
                    is the meme.

Only...
I've crossed out
some words.

I GOT ~~FINGERED ON~~ MY PERIOD ~~AND I BLOODY LOVED IT~~

My whole year
cheers and I turn around
so they can read the back:

IT'S ONLY BLOOD
#NoShame

And I get to watch
Mr Adamson's face
as he reads the front
and his eyebrows go up
but he starts nodding,
like he approves of
what he's reading.

Then Harriet throws
more spotlights on,
lighting up
Leylah,
        Bethany
                and
                        Marie,
who are joining me
on stage.

Their shirts say:
I GET MY PERIOD TOO.
IT'S ONLY BLOOD
#NOSHAME

I bite my lip to stop the grin
as Harriet lights
the whole auditorium
and I see
it's not just my friends:
loads of the girls
are wearing them.
They stand in unison
and I read the rows
in the auditorium,
saying
      over
          and over
              and over
                  again

IT'S ONLY BLOOD #NoShame IT'S ONLY BLOOD #NoShame
IT'S ONLY BLOOD #NoShame IT'S ONLY BLOOD #NoShame
IT'S ONLY BLOOD #NoShame IT'S ONLY BLOOD #NoShame
IT'S ONLY BLOOD #NoShame IT'S ONLY BLOOD #NoShame
IT'S ONLY BLOOD #NoShame IT'S ONLY BLOOD #NoShame
IT'S ONLY BLOOD #NoShame IT'S ONLY BLOOD #NoShame
IT'S ONLY BLOOD #NoShame IT'S ONLY BLOOD #NoShame
IT'S ONLY BLOOD #NoShame IT'S ONLY BLOOD #NoShame

And it was.
It was only blood.

Then I notice
that a few people
have made their
own #NoShame T-shirts,
and have put them on
over their uniforms.

Jasmine's says:
**I'M STILL A BELIEBER.
#NOSHAME**

Lee's says:
**I THOUGHT A BLOW JOB
MEANT YOU BLOW ON IT.
#NOSHAME**

Dev's says:
**I PICK MY NOSE
AND EAT IT.
#NOSHAME**

Charlie's says:
**I ONCE ACCIDENTALLY
ATE DOG FOOD.
#NOSHAME**

Then Michael Li
takes off his hoody.
His T-shirt says:
**I'M GAY.
#NOSHAME**

and a few people laugh
because he's been out
since year one.

I scan the crowd for Benjamin.
I find him.
He's crouching,
writing something
on a shirt.

He pulls it on
and it takes a moment
for everyone to realize
there's a new one.

**I ASKED MY SISTER
IF IT WAS OK
TO FINGER MY GIRLFRIEND
ON HER PERIOD.
#NOSHAME**

Benjamin raises his eyebrows,
like he's checking to see
if it's OK with me
that he called me
his girlfriend.

                                    I melt a bit
                            and smile at him,
                                        nodding.

And Benjamin grins at me.

Harriet walks onto the stage
to stand beside me.

"Oh my God,"
she whispers.
"Benjamin's T-shirt!
Cringe."

But then she adds,
"He's very sweet."

She pulls off
her own sweater.
Her floral shampoo smell
surrounds me,
which only makes it funnier
when I look down
and read her T-shirt:

**I POOED
ON THE FLOOR
IN ASSEMBLY
IN YEAR TWO.
#NOSHAME**

I think I would read a thousand
abusive DMs for just *one*
assembly like this
where we're all
laughing together.

It's not as though by
being open all
the shame goes away,
but laughing about it
somehow seems

to take some of its
power away.

And right now,
I don't feel even slightly
ashamed.
I just feel
#Happy.

I glance over at Mr Adamson
clapping along with everyone.
He looks at me,
and he directs his applause
at me, nodding and smiling.

Everyone is
whooping
and cheering
with their phones out
filming,
and Harriet puts
her arm around me
and I squish her to me,
feeling her warmth
spread over me:
a thermic reaction,
generating laughter
instead of friction.

Then Harriet whispers to me,
"Shall I do it now?"

And I look at Mr Adamson
to check he's watching.
He's still clapping,
nodding,
loving the student-led
initiative
we're showing.

I nod, my stomach wriggling.

"And one more thing,"
Harriet shouts
towards Mr Adamson.

Then she points at Jackson,
and says, "He made the meme."

I don't want to
humiliate Jackson
(I sort of do)
but I do want something
to happen to him.
I want him to be made
to understand.

"Shut up!" shouts Jackson.
"It wasn't me."

"You know it was," she says.

"Prove it!" he snarls,
looking to Dev for solidarity.

But Dev shakes his head,
and moves himself
a little away.

Then Harriet peels off
her T-shirt,
revealing another one
underneath.

**THESE ARE JACKSON
TWIGGER'S FINGERS.
#HEMADETHEMEME**

Then she turns around
to show the back,
where she's printed the evidence.
    The GPS location
    from the fingers picture
    showing it was taken
    at Jackson's address.

"Oh, fuck off," shouts Jackson.
"Everyone shared it—"

"JACKSON TWIGGER!"
bellows Mr Adamson,
making Jackson jump.
"This is not funny.
You will come with me
immediately after assembly.

If you did
what they say you did,
this will be taken
very
very
seriously."

AFTER ASSEMBLY

Everyone files out of
assembly chatting excitedly,
and some come over
to tell us how much
what we just did
meant to them.

I look at my friends
as we stand in a circle:
the five of us united
by the power of
telling our story
in our own words.

Then through the crowd
I spot Mr B smiling,
looking awkward but proud.
He walks over
to where me and Harriet
are standing chatting
with the girls.

"Well done, all of you,"
he says, beaming.
"Periods are just biology."
But he goes a bit red

and I try not to catch
anyone's eye,
because I can feel

the whole group
resisting the urge
to start giggling,
which would totally ruin
our whole point.

But Marie saves us all,
saying, "Thanks, sir."

Then Mr B says,
"Frankie," and his tone
changes as he says earnestly,
"what you did in there
was really brave.
It might not be obvious,
but bravery is something
every brilliant scientist needs."

"Thank you, sir," I say.
And I mean it.
I think I'm going to cry.

"Your essay was brilliant.
Let me know what the
planetarium say, won't you?"

"Yes, sir," I say,
nodding and remembering
my soggy application.

"And keep ignoring
those idiots online,"
he adds, going back

to usual, jokey Mr B.
"Remember the universe
is made of
protons, neutrons, electrons
and morons. Ha ha."
Then he walks away,
still laughing at his own joke.

> I bite my lip then turn
> to Harriet and whisper,
> "I threw my
> application away."

"What?" she says,
looking horrified.

> "The deadline is today.
> Did you get yours in?"

"I'm not applying."

> "Why not?" I ask.

"Because my heart isn't in it.
I don't really want it.
I'm going for this
photography thing instead.
But you *have* to apply.
Do you still have your essay?"

> "It's all on my email,"
> I say, mentally checking

the bits I'd need
to send to Vidhi.

"Then let's go!" she orders.
"Do it now while you're on
a winning streak!"

"OK!" I say,

as Harriet grabs me
and drags me
towards the computer labs.

It's amazing how uplifting
and empowering
having my best friend
beside me can be.

NORMAL GIRLS

At the end of the day,
after the meeting,
where Mr Adamson
gave us time
and space to properly explain
to Jackson
what he actually did to me,
and to Harriet too,
and to all the girls
to some extent,
we're finally free.

We follow
our parents out
of Mr Adamson's office,
Jackson and his parents
right behind us.

We turn one way,
and his family turn the other.
We've seen and said enough.
I'm just happy it's over.

Harriet and I tell our parents
we're walking home together
and we'll see them later.
As we say goodbye,
Dad pats me on the shoulder

and I try to ignore
that he's still being weird.

"Well, that went well,"
Harriet says,
her glee at her
freedom
flying off her
like subatomic particles,
invisibly influencing me.

"Jackson is angelic
in front of his parents!"

"I know, right?" she says.
"Who was that kid?"

"So quiet.
So humble.
So polite."

"Yes, Mum.
No, Dad.
I'm sorry I let you down, Mum."

"Do you think they'll actually
take his phone away?"

"I hope so," she says.
"And I'm glad he's suspended.
Mr Adamson's right:

he's lucky we're not
involving the police."

                                        "I never thought
                                        I'd hear you say
                                Mr Adamson is right."

"I never thought I'd hear
you admit you
think Benjamin
is fit."

                                                "I haven't."

"You don't need to.
He was very sweet
in assembly. You really
like him, don't you?"

                                        "I do," I say.
                                "But it's still so awkward.
                                We've hardly spoken
                                since … well, you know,
                        my period started on him.
                        And then he ignored me
                                        for a week."

We're right outside the bakery
and Harriet stops me,
her eyes wide,
her mouth open.
"Wait," she says,
a smirk on her cheeks.

"You came on him,
then you
came *on*
on
him?"

          "Shh!" I hiss, nodding, shoving
               her shoulder with mine
          and realizing that we've never
     actually talked about the details.

               But she doesn't seem
          to think it's disgusting,
               more entertaining
                    if anything.

"Oh my God!"
she practically screams.
"This is never gonna
grow old."

Inside the bakery
we get pastries,
and as we wait
for our change,
I can feel
Harriet's shoulders
still shaking
against mine.

               Out on the street,
                    walking home
          in the afternoon sun,

just two normal girls
eating croissants,
I could cry with relief.

My best friend is beside me
laughing about something
that previously
made me feel so disgusting.
#FriendsAreAmazing

"I can't really call you
a nun any more,
can I?" says Harriet.

"Nuns have periods too,
Harry," I say, then snort.

And Harriet snorts too,
which makes me laugh.
And before we know it
we're both
cackling,
laugh-crying,
gasping for breath,
tears rolling down our cheeks.

We only stop
when we get to our street
and I realize that my guts
have stopped squirming,
and, for the first time
since this all started,
I feel like myself again.

Maybe laughing
is the antidote
to shame.

"Was it good?" Harriet asks.

"Honestly?" I pause. "Yes.
Do you think that's weird?"

"No," she says.
"I think it's great."

"Do you think it's normal
that I came on … when…?"

"I expect so. If you poke it
and there's something
waiting to come out …
it's going to come.
Excuse the pun."

"Harriet! You make
everything disgusting!"

"That's why you love me,"
she says, brushing flakes
off her lips.

Then, as I'm in
a confessional mood,
I say, "I bit his thigh."

I wait, enjoying her face.

"It was
unbelievably
meaty."

DAD

Harriet and I lie
on the floor in my room
talking about
the lunar eclipse,
which is tonight.
A blood moon.
#TotallyCosmic

And we watch one of the
videos on her phone
that someone took
of us in assembly.

We're amazing.
We're warriors.
We totally nailed it.

We relive every tiny detail,
and try to take in
the bigger picture.
The hilarious expression
on Mr Adamson's face
when he read my T-shirt,
and the possibility
that what we did
might make a difference
to somebody.

Then there's a gentle knock
on my door

                                    and I sit up and say,
                                            "Hello?"

and Dad pokes his head
inside, sheepishly, saying,
"Is there room for three?"

Harriet nods
and shuffles over,
patting the floor
between us.

Dad reaches into
his back pocket
and says, "I got this
fixed for you."

                                    "My phone!"
                        Its shiny screen is mended.
                            My fingers long for it,
                    and I reach out and take it.

                                        "I love you,"
                                    I say, cradling it.

"You're talking to the phone,
aren't you?" says Dad.

                                        "Yup." I nod.

"What are you watching?"
he asks.

                              "A video of the assembly."

Dad leans in and says,
"Great. I want to see."

                              I'm not sure
                         if I want him watching

but Harriet's already
pressing *play*,

                         and although I feel
                       hot with embarrassment
                         at least there's nothing
                              invented on here.
                     It can't be more embarrassing
                       than what he's already seen.
                         This is all *real me*.

Dad watches, nodding,
and when it finishes
he says, "YES! EXACTLY!"
Then he looks at me.
"You said it, girl!"

                              I'm so shocked,
                              all I can say is
                                   "What?"

"You did. You said it.
You go, girl."

"Dad!" I groan, cringing,
"Don't call me *girl*."

"Should I call you
a woman now?"

"Ew, no,"
I cry, but I'm so relieved
that he agrees
with what we said.
"Just be normal."

"No, thank you!" he scoffs.
"Normal is boring.
I'd rather be like you."

"I thought you were
ashamed of me."

"How could I be?"

"Because of what I did."

"You didn't do anything.
I mean, I'd rather not know
the details, but that's my beef.
I'm not ashamed of you.
I never could be."

"I thought you thought
I was disgusting."

"No," he says, touching
my cheek tenderly.
"*Society* is disgusting.
You are amazing.
You have amazed me
every day since the moment
you were born.
I've never been prouder."

"Dad, are you crying?"

"Maybe," he says,
his voice wobbling,
tears brimming.

"You two are so cute!"
Harriet cries, throwing
her arms around both of us
and squeezing so tightly
we can hardly breathe.

Dad whispers,
"I love you, kid."

"I love you too,"
I say, and I'm glad
for the tight squeeze,
because I'm also crying.
Then I add, quietly,
"By the way,
I sort of have a boyfriend."

And Dad laughs hotly
into my ear
and whispers, "Well,
that's just lovely."

BLOOD MOON

Up in the tree house
Harriet and I
wait for night.
I feel floaty.
Mum was right,
being brave
really can make
your problems
melt away.
#NoWorries

I peel and portion
a tangerine and
share it with Harriet,
watching the darkness
come alive with
the light of a million stars.

We chat about the application
and what we're going to do
with our lives,
looking at the stars
and the moon rise,
the shadow of the earth
making its path
across a glowing surface.

I say,
"I think tonight

is our night for the best
moon picture yet!"

Harriet says,
"There she is!"
            pointing at me.

                                    "Huh?"

"You're back!
It's good to see you.
The good old, happy,
excited by the moon,
nerdy, wonderful you."

We set up the telescope,
watching red
seep into the moon
at its edge.
Then Harriet lines it up,
closes one eye and
puts the other
to the lens,
breathing
a long
slow
heavy
sigh.
"It's A M A Z I N G!"

I
look,
and
my mind
falls silent.

Blood red,
impossibly lustrous,
suspended over us
three hundred and eighty-four thousand
kilometres

away.

The beauty of the blood moon
reminds me that
the universe is huge
and we are tiny,
but so lucky,
because we get to
witness its beauty.

FOR EVER

I don't think
people realize that
you can take
a really good picture
of the night sky
on a phone
through a telescope.

We take a ton
and one is amazing.
Harriet posts it,
and tags me,
then we watch
the hearts come rolling in.

And I *feel* the love,
but not online.
I mean the real stuff,
right here,
from my best friend.

Although I hate
that the meme
will always be online,

it's amazing that some things
will be captured there
for all of time.

SWEET DREAMS

A noise wakes me
in the dead of night.
A scuffle,
a rustle,
the crack of a stick
underfoot.

I rub my eyes
and look at Harriet,
moonlit,
asleep beside me,
dribbling,
her phone stuck
to her cheek.

I peel it off
and place it
beside her gently,
then lean over the boards
and peer down
through the leaves.

"Psst!"
a voice hisses
on the night breeze.

Standing there,
like a dream,

beneath the dusky
green canopy,
his face lit
by the LED
of his phone screen,
is Benjamin.

"Can I come up?"
he whispers.
"I brought pastries."

I nod, but put my finger
to my lips.
"Yes, but quietly.
Harriet's asleep."

He climbs the ladder
and sits down
next to me,
smelling of his
leather jacket
and clean laundry
and the bakery.

"What time is it?"
I ask.

"It's just after three."

"What are you doing here?"
I whisper, glancing
to check Harriet's
still asleep.

"I wanted to see you,"
Benjamin says,
shuffling closer
so that both of our legs
are dangling into the tree.

                                        "How did you find me?"

"I saw Harriet's post.
That picture is *awesome*.
I remembered you said
you sometimes sleep
out here, and well,
I've been awake
watching it happen."

                                        "What happen?"
                                        I yawn, and then

he says, "Wait.
You don't know?"
He holds out his phone.

                                        "Know what?"

"I'll show you!"
he says,
placing his thumbs
over the screen excitedly.

"Your picture of
the blood moon is trending.
Look what happens
if I google you!"

Benjamin types in my name
and I wait,

      preparing for shame,
      and at the same time,
      dying to see.

He tilts his phone
to show me the first page.

And
.

.

.

The top hit
is not
the meme.

It's just the moon.
The beautiful full
glorious orb
of the blood red moon.

And the words I see

are not
           "whore"
or
     "slut"
or
         "dirty"
or
    "slag".

It's like
this
amazing picture
of the blood moon
taken on a home telescope
by two British teenagers
is
EVERYTHING.

If it keeps
trending,
this could actually
put an end to the meme.
Banish it to obscurity.

"Did your sister do this?"

He shakes his head,
smiling. "It was nothing
to do with her
or me. It was all
Harriet and you."

Benjamin looks at me
with his dimpled grin,
only this time,
there's more in there.

There's care,
and something that
feels like

being seen.

There's a crackle
between us.

And I say, honestly,
"I like your face."

He laughs and says,
"I like yours too."

"Do you want to
see the moon?
It's setting soon."

"Definitely," he says.
"Will it be *totally cosmic*?"

I giggle.
"Shh! Don't wake Harriet."

We shuffle
to the telescope,
and I adjust it to face
the full moon,
drifting down
towards the horizon.

Benjamin breathes in,
sharply, as he takes it in,
because that's what
happens when you
see something
awe-inspiring.

When he's seen
        and seen
        and seen
            he turns to me

                    his eyes shining.

                "What do you think?"
                I ask him
and he says,
    "Beautiful,"

            in a way
        that makes me think
            he's
            maybe
        talking about me.

        "Um … Frankie?"
        he says, a bit shyly.
        "Do you think
        you'd maybe want to,
            like,
        go out with me?"

        "Hmm," I say,
        pretending to think.
        "Maybe. Let's see."

OUR UNIVERSE

As dawn is breaking,
Benjamin leaves.
"I've got rugby training
before school,"
he says.

                            "So, now?" I say,
                            looking at the time
                            as he climbs down
                                    the ladder.

                    He waves, and grins,
            then walks across the grass.
        I turn around to lie back down
and Harriet is wide awake,
her face right in mine,
doing a massive
stupid
comedy
grin.

                            "HARRIET!" I shriek.
                            "Have you been awake
                                this whole time?"

"YES," she says.
"And I heard
  everything.
'I like your face.'"

I pick up my pillow
and whack her with it.
"Why didn't
you say you were
bloody awake?"

"Because," she says,
winking at me, "I know
when a girl needs *space*.
Although, my God,
the noises …
so sloppy…"

I put my hands to
my red cheeks.
"I'm so embarrassed!"

"Oh, don't be." She grins.
"You two are very cute."

"Ugh," I groan.
"I can't believe you.
You're so sneaky!"

"I know!" she says proudly,
picking up her phone.
"Anyway. I practically squealed
when I heard what he said.
I thought he was
never going to leave."

She thrusts her phone
in front of me.

"We've got loads of
new followers!"

                                              "Amazing!"

"And look…
We've got a message
from Vidhi!
The planetarium want
you and me to write a blog
for their website about
taking home-astronomy
photographs!"

                                    "That's so cool!" I say.

"And Vidhi says
you should check
your personal email,"
Harriet adds,
nudging me.

                                         I open my email
                                 and with trembling fingers
                                  find the one from Vidhi.

                              I go quiet while I'm reading
                            and I can hear Harriet breathing,
                                                    waiting.

                                   Vidhi says they're sorry
                                     they suspended me.

That it wasn't fair
and that Elaine hopes
I'll come back ASAP.

Then I read the end of her email
and I don't know whether
I'm going to laugh
or cry
or scream.

I look at Harriet,
who is watching me,
bursting.

"She's read my application.
She says it's amazing.
I have an interview next week!"

"Of course you do!"
Harriet screams.
"Oh, I absolutely
knew you would!"

And although she's still
in her sleeping bag,
she dives at me,
crashing into me,
pinning me
to the warming boards
of the tree house floor,
hugging me.

Then she moves
away from me,
her freckled nose wrinkling.
"You smell of boy."

                                                    "I do not," I say.

"Well, you smell
of *something*.
How was the kissing?"

                                        I can't help smiling.
                                            "It was amazing."

"At least he brought these,"
she says, opening
the bag of pastries
and helping herself.
"He's all right with me."

Harriet smiles at me across
a fresh dawn sunbeam
and in that moment,
I see my funny,
lovely
best friend
in all her freckled beauty.

It is a moment
overflowing with
possibility.

And right now,
right here,
with the chorus of dawn
in our sycamore tree,
that possibility is
simply
Harriet and me.

ACKNOWLEDGEMENTS

Thanks first to my passionate, meticulous editors Denise Johnstone-Burt, Megan Middleton and Susan Van Metre – it has been such a pleasure to work with you on this book; to Grainne Clear for her sharp editorial eye, Georgie Hookings for making an art form out of copy-editing, Anna Robinette for the beautiful type-setting and Jenny Bish for proofreading. Thank you to Maria Soler Canton and Laurissa Jones for the gorgeously menstrual cover, and to the wider team at Walker Books for championing this book as it goes out into the world.

To my fabulous agent, Rachel Mann, thank you for your unflinching faith in *Blood Moon* from the moment we met – I am so lucky to work with you; and thank you to Jo Unwin and the whole team at JULA for such a warm welcome.

Jo Nadin, you brilliant woman, thank you for being an extraordinary tutor. Without you this book literally wouldn't exist. You put unapologetically high expectations on me, and taught me to be bold, brave and better. I'll never forget that. Heartfelt thanks to Steve Voake, C.J. Skuse, Lucy Christopher, Janine Amos, Julia Green, David Almond and all my classmates on the MA in Writing for Young People at Bath Spa.

Thanks to my friends, particularly my writer friends Emma Levey, Angharad James, Susanna Bailey and Yasmin Rahman, who read this as it grew and told me kindly what to keep and what to delete; and most particularly to Hana Tooke, Wibke Brueggemann and Rachel Huxley – you know what you did.

I am indebted to Caitlin Williams and her friends for letting me into their teenage world; to Caroline Ambrose and the junior judges at the Bath Children's Novel Award for their passionate responses to the book; to Briony Goffin and Amanda Rackstraw for being brilliant teachers; to Katherine Judge for being an unofficial mentor, champion and dear friend; and to Sarah Crossan, Louise O'Neill, Jason Reynolds and E. Lockhart for writing the kinds of YA books that made me want to write them too.

I owe a debt to Jon Ronson for his book *So You've Been Publicly Shamed*, and to Brené Brown whose insightful work on shame informed the emotional core of this story. I also owe this book to the work of so many amazing feminists, from writers, teachers and activists, to friends, family and colleagues.

Thanks finally to my family: to Mum for talking to me about feminism from the start; to Dad who is funnier than Frankie's dad without even trying; to my sisters for being warm, witty and incredibly smutty; to the Crawford family for being so loving and supportive; and to my children for their endless appetite for stories. The biggest thanks to my husband, Will, for always believing I could do this. Listen carefully, I shall say this only once: you were right.

BLOOD MOON is Lucy Cuthew's debut novel. It is inspired by her experience of having endometriosis, which still takes an average of eight years to diagnose, despite affecting 1 in 10 women. Lucy hopes to encourage conversations about menstruation and to break down the outdated taboo around periods. The novel brings together her research on shame and the way men and women are treated differently online with her love of verse.

Lucy is a graduate of the Bath Spa MA in Writing for Young People, where she wrote *Blood Moon*. The novel was shortlisted for the Bath Children's Novel Award. She is the author of more than thirty books for younger children. She regularly speaks on the BBC about children's books and current affairs, and she runs creative writing workshops in secondary schools.

Lucy lives in Cardiff and is currently writing her second verse novel about the effects of porn on young people. When she is not writing, she enjoys listening to science podcasts and sharing Frankie and Harriet's love of croissants.

Enjoyed **BLOOD MOON**?
We'd love to hear your thoughts.

#BloodMoon
@WalkerBooksUK
@WalkerBooksYA
@LucyCuthew